WAITING FOR DADDY CHRISTMAS

A DADDY MPREG CHRISTMAS GAY ROMANCE

LORELEI M. HART

ARIA GRACE

SURRENDERED PRESS

CONTENTS

1

NOAH

I used to love Christmas.

As a kid, there was nothing better in those weeks just before Christmas, when the ground was covered in snow and the buildings and trees were draped in colored lights...and everyone was happy. Once I became an adult, I guess I understood on an intellectual level that people weren't all gumdrops and candy canes the way they appeared.

The holidays brought a lot of pain and grief and regret with them for so many people.

But it wasn't until this year, right now, that I could truly comprehend what that all meant.

Because this was the first time in my life I was dreading the last month of the year. There was nothing happy or joyous or worth celebrating in my future. Not my immediate future and not any time after that. Because for the first time in my life, I was alone. More alone than any human ever should be. Not because I was still looking for happiness. That would be so much less tragic than my reality.

I was alone because the man I loved, the alpha I promised to adore and support until my dying breath, passed away first. Not just first but way too soon. And though it had been more than eight months since his accident, I was no closer to being okay than I had been on the day I got the call from the highway patrol.

The stack of cards collecting on my dining table should have brought me some joy because I used to love getting photo holiday cards from my friends and family. But I just couldn't conjure that kind of excitement this time. All I saw when I looked at the chubby babies and loving couples was the future that was taken from me.

The future I'd never have.

My phone rang and my brother's face flashed across the screen. I considered ignoring it but knew he'd just keep calling until I answered, so I took a deep breath and hit the answer button. "Hey, Matt."

"Noah, my man, what's the word?"

"All is good here." My voice sounded unnaturally upbeat, which was my first mistake. Scratch that. Answering the call was my first mistake. "What's up with you?"

He exhaled loudly. "Don't bullshit me, Noah. I know you're not all good. And being alone in that big, empty house isn't good for you either."

"I'm not great, Matt, but I'm doing okay. And getting better every day." Lying was never my thing, but I'd become better at it over the recent months. "Really, I'm fine."

"Well, you can prove that to me when you come to our place for Christmas." Here we go. The umpteenth Christmas sympathy invite of the week. "Come up a few days early so you can hang with the kids and stay through New Year's Day. We're doing our usual Ball Drop party and there will be several single alphas there so it'll be a good chance to meet some people."

This was even worse than I thought.

"Matt, you know I love you, and I appreciate the thought." I swallowed hard and then cleared my throat. "But I'm not coming this year. I'm just not ready."

"Nope, not gonna let you sit around at home and mope. We'll see you a few days before Christmas Eve at the latest."

"Actually, I already—" I tried to feed him another lie but he hung up too quickly.

That was fine with me. He probably knew I wasn't gonna make it, so I'd just send a text the day before and claim to have the flu. That worked every time.

For about an hour, I thought I was in the clear.

And then my phone blew up and practically everyone I'd ever met was trying to get me to spend the holidays with them. It was sweet. Thoughtful. I even appreciated it. But it was completely unnecessary. I wasn't some loser omega who needed pity attention. I was a grieving man who just wanted to be left alone to think about the good times.

What was so bad about that?

My phone rang again, and this time it was my neighbor, Greg. He invited me to his weekly poker game but I only attended once every few months when I had no way of avoiding him. "Hey, Greg."

"Noah, hey. Got a sec?"

This was a trick question. If I said yes, he might invite me to hang out. Or worse, invite himself over for a beer or to watch a game. But if I said no, he would want to know what I was doing and if he could come over later, so it was easier to just get this over with. "Yeah, sure. What's up?"

"What are your plans for Christmas?"

Oh, great. Not him too. "Um, actually..." I had to make this good. I couldn't use the flu since it would be gone by Christmas. "I'm heading up to the mountains. Got a little cabin to, uh, do some meditating. My therapist thought it would be good for me."

Technically, none of that was true, but I was backed into a corner and had to say something.

"You are?" He paused for a second and then his voice perked up. "Hey, that's great. For both of us."

I was suddenly regretting my attempt at a lie, but I wasn't sure why. "How's that?"

"Well, I think it's great that you're getting out of town. You need a change of scenery. Get away from all the ghosts that haunt you."

"Um, yeah, I guess." I wouldn't call the memory of the only man who had ever loved me a *ghost,* but I didn't have the energy to argue with him. "So how is that good for you?"

"Well, my sister's family is surprising us by coming into town for Christmas, and my parents are already gonna be here so..."

Shit. I could already tell where this was going.

"If your place will be empty, can I maybe rent it or something? That way my sister and her annoying husband can be close but not too close?"

"Oh, right." Think. Think. Think. "I can't really think of a reason to say no..." Even though I really wanted to.

"Cool. Thanks, man! We appreciate it."

I sighed heavily. "Of course. No worries." Apparently, I needed to find a place to stay for Christmas so I could avoid seeing all the people who loved me. This was why I hated to lie. "Happy I could help."

As soon as I got off the phone with Greg, I grabbed my laptop and a beer and plopped down on the sofa. What were the chances I could find a secluded cabin to rent at Christmas time with minimal notice and within my nonexistent budget?

Yeah, that was what I was afraid of.

2

CRUZ

I stared at the contract for a full minute before I finally hit the button to electronically sign it and then submit it to the contractor. Switching the entire electrical system over to solar was an expensive upgrade, but I knew it would pay off in the long run. Unfortunately, in the short run, I was emptying my savings account to make it happen. There wasn't much left for an emergency, but my vacation rental was booked through New Year's at the prime holiday rate. As long as no checks bounced, my bank account would have a buffer again in no time.

As soon as the contract was submitted, I stepped into my running shoes to brave the frigid weather for a quick run. Running had always been my way of letting off pent-up tension, stress, or excitement. I wasn't sure I could identify just one of those emotions, but I definitely needed to stretch my legs and get some fresh air.

The cold air felt like sharp spikes poking my lungs. It only took a few minutes of heavy panting for my whole body to warm up, and then each breath I sucked in was refreshing.

Excitement.

That was what I was feeling. I was excited about the future and about finally having a season in the green. When I bought the cabin three years ago, I had big plans for it. But every upgrade I made led to five issues being revealed. Now that the cosmetic improvements were all done, the money coming in was all gravy.

I finished a five-mile loop then slowed to a walk to cool down.

My foot had just landed on the first step to my porch when I got an alert from the reservation system I used to handle the bookings. "Sweet, another fat check coming in."

With a smile on my face, I opened up the booking app as I pushed open the back door and went inside. "Let's see how much money I just made."

Usually, there was a green dollar sign in the upper corner of the app when a new reservation was made. But I didn't see the dollar sign. Instead, I saw a red frowny face. "What the hell is this?"

I kicked the door shut and zoomed in to read the message next to the unfamiliar icon. "Reservation cancelled?" I scrolled down to see which booking was trying to cancel. It was common practice to offer a 14-day cancellation window without penalty, so I didn't think anything of using that as my standard policy. But when I saw that the reservation backing out was for twelve days, ending on January first, I almost threw my phone across the room in frustration. "Fuck!" That was my gravy train right there. The nightly rate was tripled during that week, and there was basically zero chance I could find someone to rent the cabin for that rate on such short notice. "There goes my fucking slush fund."

After a quick shower to rinse off, I got over my pity party and grabbed my computer. I might not be able to replace the entire booking, but maybe I could get a family in for a few days around Christmas and then another group for New Year's. It wasn't ideal and would probably only bring in a fraction of what I was banking on, but it was better than nothing.

With low expectations and few options, I posted links to the rental site on all my social media accounts. Maybe a friend of a friend would see it and decide to be spontaneous. Or better yet, maybe a family with a bunch of kids who loved playing in the snow would decide to chase a white Christmas this year.

As soon as the posts were live, I put my computer away and turned on the TV. I wasn't a big TV guy, but it was a great distraction. And with all the new worries racing through my mind, a distraction was exactly what I needed.

Just as I was getting sucked into an old episode of Three's Company, my phone rang. I hoped the family who cancelled was calling to uncancel, but when I saw the area code on my phone, I knew it wasn't them. But it wasn't anyone in my contacts either.

"Hello, this is Cruz."

A soft cough was followed by a throat being cleared before there was finally a voice at the other end of the line. "Hi, um, I'm calling about the cabin for rent."

Oh, maybe it was my lucky day. "Okay, cool. Well, it's still available. What days are you looking for?"

"Christmas Eve and Christmas Day for sure. Maybe a few days before and after." He cleared his throat again and then sighed. "But, um, I wasn't able to get to the website to see the price. How much is it per night?"

"Six hundred a night from the twenty-third through January third. One eighty per night the rest of the time."

"Oh." I could hear the disappointment in the man's voice with just the single syllable. "Sorry to bother you, but that's outside of my budget."

Before I could offer him a discount or find out what his budget was, he disconnected the call. "Dammit. What's going on today?" I hit the call-back button and leaned back on the sofa. Clearly, I wasn't meant to have money.

The phone only rang once before the timid man answered again. "Hello?"

"This is Cruz again. You just called about my cabin."

"Yeah." He seemed terrified, but I'd hoped it was for other reasons. "Can I help you?"

I shrugged, even though he couldn't see me. "I don't know. What's your name?"

"Noah, why?" He was less timid when he was suspicious, and it sounded like he was suddenly very suspicious. "Why are you calling?"

Why was I calling? To beg him to find more money? "What's your budget for the cabin?"

He was quiet for a few seconds, as if he didn't know how to respond. "Like five hundred bucks, total. I'm sorry for wasting your time, it's just that this year has been really bad for me and..." He paused and then sniffled as if he might be crying. "Anyway, it doesn't matter. Just forget I called."

I could tell he was about to hang up, but I stopped him in time. "Whoa there. Just hold on a sec. What happened this year?" It was absolutely none of my business and yet I couldn't ignore the pain I heard in his voice.

"Well, if you must know, my alpha died." He sucked in a deep breath then blew it directly into the mic of his phone. "This is my first Christmas alone, and I just wanted to get away from my well-meaning but very intrusive family. But I can't afford a place like yours, so thanks anyway."

Well, shit. How could I ignore that? I'd always had a soft spot for people in need. Especially someone who sounded so broken and lost. "Okay."

His breathing stuttered. "Okay, what?"

"Okay, you can have the cabin for five hundred." Who needed a savings account anyway?

3

———

NOAH

Was I really doing this?

Was I actually going to head to a mountain retreat all by myself just to avoid my loved ones over Christmas?

Yes. Yes, I was.

It was pathetic, but I just couldn't bear the idea of pity looks and forced conversation with people who were "just trying to help." I appreciated all the effort they put into making me feel better, but I just needed a little bit more time to myself.

Not too much time.

I promised myself that I'd start to move on after the holidays were over. It seemed reasonable enough, even though I had no idea how that could possibly happen. All I knew was that I couldn't continue this sad existence for much longer. Every day, it was harder and harder to get out of bed, and I knew that wasn't what Steve would have wanted for me.

He would have wanted me to mourn for a month or two and then start living my life again. In my heart, I knew that. But that same heart also refused to feel anything but lost.

"I guess this is it." I grabbed a couple books from my bookshelf and tossed them into the bag with groceries and then headed out to my car.

Greg was on his way up my driveway at the same time. "Oh, good thing I caught you. Looks like you're on your way out."

"Yeah, I was just going to head over and hand these to you." I held out a set of keys to him. "Your sister will probably need to stock the kitchen with whatever they'll want, but all the sheets have been changed, and I left instructions for accessing the Wi-Fi."

"You're a lifesaver, man. I wish you were sticking around, but getting to use your place is a huge help for us." He looked like he was about to hug me, and I definitely wasn't ready to be touched intimately by any man, especially not my neighbor.

To intercept his affection, I clapped his shoulder briefly. "No worries. Call if you need anything, but reception might not be great up in the mountains."

He stilled then took a step back, accepting my distance for what it was. "We'll be fine. You have fun too. You need it."

I almost laughed in his face, but I nodded instead. "See you in the new year."

I waited until I had backed out of my driveway and was safely on the road before I relaxed my lips, and my smile morphed into its usual frown. I hadn't always been a frowner, but there had been few opportunities to smile over the past year, so it just seemed to become my new resting face.

According to my GPS, I had a two-hour drive to the cabin ahead of me.

I actually enjoyed driving, so that wasn't the problem. The problem was the guilt I felt over taking the cabin at such a low rate. Then again, maybe it wasn't as nice as the pictures made it look to be. People used old or even fake photos of these vacation rentals all the time. Maybe this was actually a dump and I was overpaying for it.

A smirk formed on my face. *I would deserve that.*

When I finally turned off the gravel road and stopped in front of the address on my post-it note, my jaw dropped. It definitely wasn't a dump. At least from the outside, it was a nicely renovated cottage that could have housed an entire family at the nightly rate of what I was paying for ten days.

Dammit! Now I felt even guiltier.

After double-checking the address to make sure I was at the right place, I got out of the car and grabbed my bags from the backseat. Not wanting to make two trips, I tried to carry the two bags of groceries, a duffel bag of clothes, and my computer bag all at once. It worked on my way to the car, and it should have worked again. Unfortunately, this time I managed to step onto a patch of ice just a few feet away from the car, and it dropped me to my ass and had my groceries dispersed in every direction.

"Whoa there. Are you okay?" A deep voice rumbled behind me and my whole body went still. Not just from embarrassment but from a tingle that shot through me, straight from my belly. "Hold tight. Let me help."

I turned to the man who was suddenly beside me and saw that his hands were outstretched to help me up, so I instinctively reached for them. "I'm okay." That was the same lie I told everyone in general, so it was easy to spew in this situation. Mostly, I was physically okay, but there was a sharp pain in my hip that was concerning.

"Are you sure?" He pulled me to my feet then brushed some snow off my elbows. "That was a pretty good tumble you took there."

He was holding my hand, so I carefully pulled it back then brushed the snow off my ass and thighs. "Yeah, the only bruises are on my ego. Are you Cruz?"

"That's me. You must be Noah." He reached down for the bunch of bananas by his feet. "Welcome to your home away from home for the next few weeks."

"Thanks." I looked at my scattered groceries and could feel my cheeks burning even brighter red. He must've thought I was a complete fool. "Let me just grab these."

"I've got them." In the time it took me to hunt down a single can of soup that was slowly rolling toward a tree, he collected all the rest of my groceries and neatly piled them into a bag.

A single bag.

He must have been some kind of Jenga Master because I had two full bags when I arrived, and he managed to arrange everything perfectly into one.

"Wow, that's impressive." I glanced around the yard to make sure everything was picked up before reaching for my duffle bag. At least my computer bag managed to stay tucked in front of me as I fell, so it didn't have any contact with the hard ground. "Where were you when I was packing this morning?"

He was quiet for a moment, so I looked up and met his gaze. His dark eyes stared intently at me, as if he were trying to see through me. He opened his mouth to speak, but no words came out. He just reached forward for my duffle, wordlessly commanding that I hand it over.

As if I were on autopilot, I reached for the strap and handed it to him, allowing him to carry the majority of my belongings, even though I had a free hand. "You don't have to..."

His chin dropped down once in a nod, and he gestured toward the front door. "Actually, I think I do."

4
______

CRUZ

I still didn't understand what it was about him that had me practically giving Noah the room. I could tell myself that it was because I could hear the tears in his voice, but the truth was, my heart was already being tugged in his direction.

There was just something about this man that drew me to him.

Like he was a little kitten found in the snow who needed to be protected and cared for.

And then I saw him, met him for the first time face to face, scented him, and now there was more to the mix. I was attracted to him, and that was a huge pile of nope. He was a widower, his mate gone from this world.

Not to mention that he was my guest. There was no part of this scenario that was okay to be feeling, much less pursuing.

"If you need anything, here's my number." I handed him my card like it was a formal business transaction.

He flashed a shy smile. "I have it."

Duh. Of course he did. We'd talked on the phone more than once. What was wrong with me? Oh yeah, I was mesmerized by the omega's bright blue, yet sad eyes, his dimples, and his wavy hair.

This was not good. This was very not good.

Had we met in a bar, I'd have already been working on a way to get him home and in my bed. But as a guest, he was off limits, and I needed to treat him with nothing but respect. And that involved zero elements of wooing.

Wooing? I needed to get out of there.

The longer I stayed with him, the more I wanted to move in with him for his time there and take care of him. He didn't need that.

"You do." I took the card back. "It's automatic. Most people do all their bookings online."

"And pay you what it's worth," he mumbled under his breath, his guilt heavy.

"Actually, you saved me." Could I have gotten a new reservation at a higher rate? Absolutely. But I wasn't going to say that and add to his fretting. I wanted to take it away—take all of it away. "The reason I offered a discount is because I did have a reservation and they cancelled. If you hadn't taken the place, it'd be sitting empty this whole time. And since I'm working on going green, every booking helps."

His eyes lit up for the first time since he arrived. "Green? Are you going solar?"

"I am. Out here, it makes sense. We have plenty of sun, and along with the roof, I have some areas of land that will be used too. I'm pretty excited about it." Only wished it didn't cost so much for the initial investment.

He nodded, suddenly less withdrawn. "That sounds great."

My phone started to ring and it was work. Had it been anything else, I'd have ignored it. "I have to take this. Call me if you need anything." I walked out, answering the phone as I went. It was rude to let a call interrupt our conversation, but maybe that was good.

If he thought I was rude, maybe that would help stem this attraction I felt.

Even dealing with a work fiasco, my mind wasn't far from the omega with the sad eyes. When I took him some kindling the next morning and he was sitting at the window, watching the flurries of snow, I knew I had to do something.

Spending his Christmas holiday in lonely misery wasn't what I wanted for him or anyone.

I walked up to the door with little kindling candle cups and knocked. A plan was already forming in my head on how to cheer him up. He needed more than just some isolated time away from everything. Noah needed to experience some joy this season, and fuck me, I needed to give that to him. I couldn't just ignore the omega. He deserved better.

I didn't even know what made me so sure of that, but I was.

"Hello? Is everything okay?" He opened the door, his eyes red.

Shit, he'd been crying. "I brought these for the fireplace. A woman at the local Christmas fair makes them and they work well."

"Thanks." He smiled sweetly up at me after taking a look at the little cups. "They look too pretty to burn."

"Are you ready?" And operation "make-the-omega's-Christmas-one-to-remember" was officially in force.

He raised an eyebrow and cocked his head. "For?"

"It's time for the Christmas tree, of course?"

He fumbled with the kindling candles I'd given him, looking both confused and excited.

"It's part of the booking? Your cozy mountain Christmas package?"

His eyes went wide like he had no idea what I was talking about. And he didn't, since I'd just made it up on the spot.

"Every day, you get a different Christmas experience, and today's experience is getting a tree?" I made it a question so he could feel like he was part of the decision. I felt shitty lying to him, but I doubted he'd agree to doing anything if he didn't feel somewhat obligated.

"But I didn't even pay full price." Apparently, that was the excuse he'd use since he didn't want to go.

"Pissh. They are all pre-arranged, so we might as well use them." I needed to text Fran at the Christmas tree farm to let her know to bill me so Noah wouldn't feel worse. We could just get one from the land, but there was something magical about the farm, and Fran's family could use the small boost in income.

He sighed and then nodded. "Okay. When do we leave?"

"Now?"

I caught a brief smile before he raced off to get ready while I messaged Fran.

When we arrived, she had a special tour of the farm all set up, including a horse-drawn sleigh ride to the river, a cocoa and cookie break, and the tree-cutting experience. She was amazing. It was like she knew with a simple text of ***Bringing someone to get a tree. Bill me because…Christmas*** that I wanted this to be special.

We had a great time, and each smile Noah gave felt like a victory.

I learned so much about him during the short afternoon we'd spent together. He loved chocolate and preferred whipped cream to marshmallows on his cocoa. Noah also adored horses. Of the entire sleigh-ride experience, feeding apples to Dasher and Fred, the two horses pulling our sleigh, was the highlight for him. Not to mention that Noah took picking a Christmas tree very seriously.

"I've never had a real tree before." He put his hands on his hips and admired the tree again after we loaded it into the back of my truck. "Thank you for this. It's like Christmas, but a new way of doing it."

"I'm glad you enjoyed it. Fran's farm is one of my favorite places this time of year." And in all honesty, this afternoon had been one of the best ones I'd had in a very long time.

He glanced back at the orchard of trees. "I can see why. It means a lot that you've shared it with me."

"It came with the cabin rental," I lied, the words sour in my mouth. I didn't want to admit the feelings that had been stirred up today, and I for sure didn't want to make him feel pitied. He deserved so much better.

Better than a liar? Shit. Maybe I needed to be honest with him.

That was actually...fun. Like, really fun.

I was hesitant to go out alone with Cruz, but I was really glad I did. Not only did he make me feel somewhat normal again, but he looked at me as a normal person. Not a person who should be pitied or given special treatment because of my loss, but just as a man. A friend.

And I hadn't felt that since Steve.

Just that thought made me feel guilty for comparing Cruz to Steve. But that wasn't what today was about. At least, I didn't think that was the case. Cruz was just a good host who was trying to earn a four-star review since he wasn't getting his full rate for the cabin.

I didn't blame him for that. And maybe he was a little bit lonely too.

When we got back to the cabin, I expected Cruz to bring the tree inside and then take off, but I should have known better. He did bring it inside and set it up next to the loveseat underneath the front window. But he wasn't done yet. "What do you think?"

I took a few steps back and looked at the branches in all directions. "There's a little bit of a bald spot in that corner." I pointed toward the lower left edge of the tree.

Cruz nodded. "Yeah, I see it." He reached between the branches and grabbed the trunk, giving it a subtle rotation. "How's that?"

I cocked my head and nodded. "It's perfect. Looks amazing."

"It is perfect," he said quietly.

When I glanced toward him, I noticed he wasn't looking at the tree. He was staring straight at me. A flush crept up my neck, and I quickly turned away, not sure how to respond. Biologically, I wanted to run into his arms and relieve some of the tension I'd been feeling between us all day, but I knew I couldn't do that. And in my head, I knew I shouldn't do that.

It wasn't right. I should still be in mourning.

"Well, um." I slipped my hands in my pockets and kept my gaze locked on the tree. "Thanks for helping me pick it out."

"Yeah, I guess I should—" He stopped short, his head frantically looking around the room. "Ornaments. I forgot to pick up ornaments."

"Oh... That's okay. It looks great as it is."

"Nonsense. We can't have a naked tree in here."

My eyes went wide and the flush crept even higher.

"You know what I mean." He chuckled. "Maybe we can find some stuff around here to make some?" He looked around at the bookshelves. There wasn't a lot to work with. "I know there's popcorn in the pantry. And I have an old sewing kit around here somewhere. Didn't they used to make garland out of strings of popcorn?"

I smiled. "Yeah, my grandma used to do that when we were kids."

"Great. And there's a box of craft paper around here somewhere. Maybe we can cut out some colorful ornaments and attach them with yarn." He laughed out loud now. "It might look a little janky, but it'll be fun putting it all together."

I couldn't help chuckling too. He just made me feel lighter. "Yeah, that will be fun."

After a bit of hunting, we settled in at the coffee table to work on our decorations.

I'd always enjoyed crafting, but this felt different than just making cute greeting cards for relatives. This felt almost intimate. Like Cruz and I were doing something a family would do together.

And that made my belly flutter. The funny thing was, I was familiar with the flutter. It wasn't the flutter that happened when I felt sad or worried. It was the flutter that happened when I was excited. Happy. It was the same flutter I felt when I met Steve.

After cutting out a pile of random shapes and taping yarn hooks to them, Cruz placed a big bowl of popcorn on the table between us and handed me a spool of thread and a needle. "I don't know if there's a trick to this, but I think we literally just poke through the middle of each kernel until we run out of thread or popcorn."

"That sounds about right to me." I pulled a long length of thread from the spool then shoved the end through the eye of the needle.

We got to work, and it almost became a competition to see who could make the longest string. We joked and made up silly Christmas songs while we worked, and by the time we ran out of popcorn, we had almost fifteen feet of garland for the tree.

Cruz attached our ends of string together then handed it all to me. "You can do the honors."

"How about we do it together?" I bit my lip and glanced up at him.

Cruz swallowed hard and nodded. "Okay."

Without another word, I grabbed one end and tucked it into the back of the tree, then we carefully draped it along the branches, spiraling from the bottom up until we got to the top.

There was only about two feet of string left when the branches were out of my reach. "Can you finish the top?"

"Of course." Cruz leaned forward and gently placed the last few inches of popcorn carefully across the top until the last piece was arranged at the tip. "How does it look?"

"Perfect." I echoed the word he'd used earlier, and when he caught me looking at him instead of the tree, I knew I was in trouble.

The air sizzled between us, and I think we were both unsure of how to proceed. My emotions were at war inside me, but I didn't spend too much time thinking. I just wanted to feel. Instinctively, I stepped toward Cruz and wrapped my arms around his waist, resting my cheek against his shoulder. "Thank you for today. I really needed this."

His arms closed around me and held me close. Something brushed across the top of my head but I wasn't sure if it was his nose or lips. Either way, a shiver ran down my spine and straight to my balls.

I shouldn't be there. I shouldn't be in his arms, but I couldn't step away.

Fortunately, he made the decision for me. He cleared his throat and stepped back. "I, uh, better get out of your hair. I hijacked your day, and I'm sure you'd like some rest."

"Oh. Okay." Oops. Maybe I had misread the situation. Maybe the hug was over the line. Actually, it was over the line. What was I thinking? "Yeah, I am pretty tired."

Cruz quickly cleaned up the supplies we had out then walked to the door.

I followed close behind, not sure what to say, but knowing there was so much left unsaid.

He took a step out before he stopped and turned back to me. His face was just inches from mine, and I was sure he was about to lean in for a kiss.

My eyes drifted shut, and I softly inhaled, ready to hold my breath as long as might be necessary.

But instead of his soft lips on mine, I felt his warm breath across my face. "Tomorrow is toasted marshmallows and hot cocoa night. If there's anything you need before then, just let me know."

And with that, he was gone, striding away like it was the easiest thing in the world for him to do.

I sighed and closed the door, leaning against it before sliding down to the ground. It was good that he didn't kiss me. That would have been awkward, and I wasn't sure how my body would have responded.

Okay, that was a lie.

As wrong as it may have been, I wanted it. And if he had kissed me, I would have kissed him back.

Enthusiastically.

6

CRUZ

What was I thinking?

First I hugged him and then...then I almost kissed him. And worse? He looked like he wanted me to.

The day had been so magical, as cliche as that was. It was as if the Christmas magic of books and TV specials came to life. Shit, it felt like I was in a Hallmark movie. It was no wonder we both got wrapped up in the moment. Sleigh rides and cocoa and tree decorating and the snow flurries.

It wasn't my fault. It wasn't his. I blamed Christmas.

And like any wise alpha would do...I got the hell out of there, but not without the promise of a new activity for tomorrow. Unfortunately, being a frazzled mess, I promised toasted marshmallows and cocoa. That was definitely a great treat, but was it something that would take more than an hour? Not even close.

I needed to find something else for us to do. I mean, for him to do. These activities weren't about me. Sure, I was attracted to him and I enjoyed spending time with him, but if that was all it was, I'd have done what I did with all my guests and left him alone to have his time in the woods without interference.

But it was more than that.

Even if I couldn't fully verbalize what that meant, I knew it was *more*.

My cabin wasn't far from the rental. Too far to walk in this weather, but less than a five-minute drive. I pulled in and heard the welcoming call of Autumn, my dog. She came with the name and it had caused a *Who's on First* type of conversation more than once over the years.

"I'm coming," I called to her as I got out of my truck, my boots crunching on the hard-packed snow. "Hold your horses."

And of course, that brought me back to the joy on Noah's face as he fed the horses apples earlier today. The previous owners of my place had horses when I first looked at it. I was tempted to get one myself a few times, but work had become a hot mess of long days, and I had been worried I wouldn't have enough time for them.

Now that work had settled, maybe it was time to reconsider the idea.

"Hey, sweet girl." I bent down to let my fluffy girl give me the greeting she was barking for. She was a hugger. My dog literally hugged people, legs around your neck and all. In my opinion, it was better than licking as far as habits went, but she caught a lot of people off guard, because when Autumn wanted a hug, she was right up in your business until she got one.

"I need to do some work, but after that, we can go for a walk." I scratched her head before giving her a pat.

Work took me twice as long as it should've with my mind constantly wandering back to Noah. *Did he have something for dinner? Was he still smiling? What would he have done if I had kissed him?*

I found myself going straight from doing work to googling local things-to-do for Christmas. There was a great deal happening in the area but nothing suitable for the next day. Something did catch my eye, though. The local senior center had made ornament kits and was selling them as a fundraiser for their New Year's Eve Dinner Dance. From what it sounded like, the kits included everything you needed to make a dozen fancy ornaments, and who didn't want to give people a fun night out?

"How about we go for a ride, Autumn?"

She was all about that, wagging her tail and jumping up and down.

"I'll take that as a yes."

We drove into town and got to the center just as they were closing the table for the day.

"Haven't seen you in a minute." Mrs. Larson greeted me with a warm hug, wearing a Mrs. Claus apron and a huge smile. She was right, it had been a while since I'd been there. Not since my grandfather had passed. Given my greeting, I probably needed to remedy that.

"I know, but work has been...work. But, I'll be here for the cookie walk, don't you worry." Everyone in town came for the cookie walk. It was the highlight of the season. "But today, I came for some of your ornament kits."

"What kind are you interested in? Felt, glass, or possibly beads?" She held up one at a time as if she were on a home shopping television show.

"How about you make an assortment? Right now, the tree really only has paper ornaments. It needs some love."

"Speaking of love... Autumn, don't think I haven't noticed you're ignoring me." She pretended to scold my dog as she squatted down for her hug.

Autumn didn't disappoint.

After her hug, Mrs. Larson asked me what my budget was and then gleefully maxed it out with an entire box full of kits. "This should keep you busy."

"I think it will. Thanks so much. This is a great idea." And it was. People loved to craft, and buying all the separate pieces was costly if you didn't want to commit to making a ton of each kind.

"Tomorrow, we're having our candy sale." She beamed with pride. "A new sale every day. We're not messing around with this dinner dance. We're even trying to get a band this year."

I raised an eyebrow in interest. "I may be back. Do you know if there will be marshmallows? I was headed to Johnson's Grocer to grab some, but I'd rather have the good stuff."

She crooked her finger for me to come in closer, and then said softly, "I've got the goods out back. If you want to pay an 'early buyer' fee, I think I can hook you up."

I burst out in a chuckle before realizing just how serious she was. "If you can get me some divinity and fudge as well, I'll pay a premium price."

"If you want Frank's famous turtles, I can get you those too."

"I'm in."

She went out back to collect my treats, and I wrote her a check for the entire amount Noah had given me. Fuck the slush fund. Something felt wrong about keeping that money. Maybe it was because the cancellation was just too perfectly timed with Noah needing a place to escape...his sorrow...or maybe it was the season getting to me.

Whatever it was, spending the money here felt right.

And if I got some of Frank's turtles in my belly by doing so, who was I to complain?

7

———

NOAH

Still hard.

Not only had I rubbed one out in the shower after Cruz left, but I also had to get myself off before I could fall asleep. I was sure that would be enough to make my cock relax. It was two more orgasms than I'd had in almost a year, and my body should be exhausted.

But it wasn't.

I woke up with a boner that was more than just morning wood. It was like a twenty-four-hour tree trunk that wouldn't be sated. After lying in the comfy bed for almost an hour, I decided I had to take matters into my own hands.

Again.

The fantasy wasn't one I should have been indulging in, but it was so easy to imagine Cruz actually kissing me, the way his lips would feel when they pressed against mine. I wrapped my fingers around my cock and began to stroke up and down. Each time my palm rolled over the head, a new drop of precome coated the skin, lubricating me the way my ass would lubricate Cruz's thick alpha cock.

My balls felt heavy as they drew closer to my body. They should have been empty, but just thinking about Cruz sliding his hard rod in and out of me, giving me his seed and his knot like only a true alpha could, made my body produce everything it needed to take that cock.

Over and over again.

I didn't last very long, and when I shoved three fingers into my ass, pretending it was Cruz's knot stretching me out and locking inside me, I came with a jolt and my whole body bucked off the mattress. "Cruz, yes! Take me, alpha."

I didn't move fast enough to grab a towel or shirt to come into, so the sheets were a sticky mess by the time

I was done and my cock had finally started to relax. It wasn't fully soft, and I was beginning to wonder if maybe it never would be. At least not until I'd had a real alpha claim it.

What was I saying? I didn't have a real alpha anymore. He was gone.

I sighed heavily then dragged myself out of bed. I needed to get the sheets washed and back on the bed before Cruz showed up for the marshmallow thing or I'd have a very embarrassing situation to explain.

I HAD an embarrassing situation to explain.

After spending over an hour trying to get the dryer to work, I just couldn't figure out the trick to getting it to stay on for more than a minute. It wasn't at all like the basic model I had at home. This one had some steam option and kept flashing a condensation error. I pushed every button and did everything I could think of to clear the error, but it just wasn't working.

Which left me with only one option. I had to call Cruz for help.

When he arrived at my door hours earlier than he'd planned to come by, I felt terrible. "I'm so sorry for calling. I'm usually not so high-maintenance, but I need to get these sheets dried or else I'll be sleeping on the couch tonight."

"It's okay, Noah." He held up his hands to stop me. "Just take a breath and tell me again what the problem is."

I sucked in a deep breath then blew it out. "Sorry. I just can't figure out the dryer. There's an error, and I really need to dry these before I can go to bed tonight."

"Got it." He nodded and followed me back to the closet with the washer and dryer. "I think I know what's wrong. It happens every few months, so I should have checked it before you got here." His eyes were kind as he placed his hand on my shoulder to reassure me that he wasn't angry. "This is my fault, not yours."

"Oh, okay. I'm just glad I didn't break it. It looks brand-new...and expensive."

He just smiled. "Nothing's broken, but I'm sorry you were worried about it."

Within a few minutes, he'd unscrewed a panel along the bottom and pulled out a secret tray full of water that I never would have known was there. Maybe it wasn't actually my fault after all. "So that's it?"

"Not your fault at all." He dumped the water and then got the dryer put back together. "And your, um, sheets should be dry in about an hour."

"Thanks." I avoided making eye contact, knowing I needed to explain why I washed the sheets so early in my trip, but I wasn't sure what I should say. "I was just...having a snack and I spilled some—"

"Don't, Noah." Cruz held up a hand and met my gaze. His tone was different than I'd heard before. It was lower and more...intense. "Don't make up a story for my sake. I had to change my sheets too. It's okay. It's...natural."

"Oh." I had no idea how to respond to that. Was he saying he was attracted to me too? Or just that he was a man and men made messes in their sheets? I just bit the inside of my cheek, wishing I was better able to read his mind. "Okay."

"Do you have anything going on right now? I can come back later to work on today's activities."

"No, no." I reached for his arm but stopped myself before I actually grabbed him. "I'm not busy at all, so if you want to stay, that'd be great."

He held my gaze for a moment before smiling. "Great. Then I'll just get some stuff from my truck."

I watched him go out to his truck and squealed a little when a huge, white samoyed jumped out of the cab and trotted right to my front door. Without hesitation, I pulled open the door and dropped to my knees. "Who are you, sweet girl?"

"That's Autumn." Cruz had a large shopping bag in his arms. "She's a hugger, so be careful."

When she placed her big paws on my shoulders and seemed to cling to me, I understood his warning. "Wow, she's...big."

He chuckled. "Autumn, that's enough. Let Noah breathe."

The dog backed away and followed Cruz inside the cottage. He put down his bag and began pulling out ornaments.

"Are we crafting again?" My smile was genuine as I lifted up a small bag of beads. "These are beautiful."

"Yup, this tree needs more than paper ornaments, so I thought this would be fun...and then we'll head outside to toast those marshmallows." He looked at me, stopping all movement to catch my gaze. "If that sounds good to you."

"It sounds great to me." Better than great. It sounded like the best way to spend the day. "Show me what to do."

8
———
CRUZ

"If you put a fire on, I'll make dinner." Noah went into the kitchen to wash his hands.

We'd had such an amazing day together. When he called me and said he needed my help...it hit something deep inside me. And then when I realized it was because he'd made a mess of his sheets...adorable.

I normally wouldn't have confessed anything about my alone time like that, not when we'd just met, but he needed to know it was okay.

And that was when I should've headed home.

But let's face it, there was no way I was turning down that offer, especially with that hopeful look on his face.

I couldn't remember ever having such a fun day. The last thing I wanted to do was leave his side. It wasn't even just the yearning to make his stay, his holiday, better.

Maybe—at first, it was.

But the more time I spent with Noah, the more I connected with him, and the more I just enjoyed him as an omega. And really, the more time we spent together, the more he let me see the omega he was.

"That sounds like the deal of the century." I took off my gloves and stretched my arms over my head. "I'll happily accept the offer as stated."

He gave me some skeptical side-eye, more amused than anything else. "You didn't even ask what I'm making."

"I get to set things on fire and warm my fingertips in exchange for not cooking. It's a total win no matter what we have." I left off the part about the company being the best I could remember in ages. He didn't need that pressure or awkwardness infused into what was a pretty fabulous day.

He was beaming, which seemed like a rare occasion. "Okay, then I'll get the cereal out. Is Autumn allowed to eat cereal? Not chocolate, of course."

At first, I thought he was serious with his firm and business-like tone. And if he was, I would have been fine with it. If eating cereal gave me more time with Noah, eating cereal it would be.

But then I saw the slight curve of his lips and knew he was messing with me...and I loved it.

"Autumn can't eat onions, raisins, or chocolate. And if you want to be in the same room as her, I'd highly suggest you avoid eggs as well."

Noah's mouth opened and closed as if not sure where to go from there.

"Other than that, she's fine. I'll get this fire going so mine doesn't get soggy." I turned and took one step toward the fire when he came clean.

"Actually, I was gonna make grilled cheese sandwiches and tomato soup."

"My favorite." It was all I could do not to turn around to watch his expression, but the odds were too good that it would have made me cross the room to cup his cheek and ask permission for that kiss I almost got last night.

And that would not be good.

It was getting more and more challenging to remember why it wouldn't be good, but it wouldn't be. That much I did remember.

I got the fire going, and the delicious aroma of the butter-soaked bread grilling tickled my nose. It truly was one of my favorites. There was something so comfortable and homey about a gooey grilled cheese sandwich.

The fire started easily, the flames crackling in the beautiful way that only came from natural firewood. I never understood why people used the fake ones, even though I left a few in the cabin for them, just in case.

"Fire's ready." I walked into the kitchen, expecting to see cans on the counter from the soup. Instead, there was a cutting board covered in tomato juice. "Did you make the soup? Like *make* make it?"

"I cheated a little bit. I had some stewed tomatoes in the fridge left over from last night's dinner that I started with."

Huh. My omega could cook. Well, not my omega. The omega. My guest. My guest could cook. "I'm impressed. It smells delicious." Beyond delicious. "What can I do to help?"

"The soup is almost ready, so I just need to grill the sandwiches." He reached for a plate on the counter and handed it to me. "I made this one for Autumn. It has cream cheese. My uncle used to wrap his dog's pill in cream cheese, so I figured it wasn't bad for her. I also put in some chunks of the beef I had last night."

I took the offered plate, blown away by the thoughtfulness of the dish. "Wow, you're spoiling her."

"Oh, it's okay if she can't have it. I just...she was watching me so intently with that smile. I didn't know dogs smiled."

I knew that smile oh too well. "There's no denying her anything when she looks at you with that smile. Thank you for this."

I cut Autumn's dinner into little pieces as he grilled the sandwiches he already had assembled. Not sure why I bothered cutting them up, since she was going to scarf it all down in one bite.

"I'll bring everything to the table, and you can feed her. That way she'll know her super powers work on you too." I set the plate with Autumn's food down and grabbed our bowls. It wasn't the healthiest of dinners for her, but she was happy to have it.

Autumn managed to devour it all before we sat down to our soup and sandwiches.

After sampling both, my senses were firing with pleasure. "This is good...like, really good."

"Thanks. Steve used to say the canned stuff was better." Noah stirred his soup, not looking up at me. "He didn't like any of my cooking."

"That must've been hard." What could I say to that? It wasn't like I could tell him his alpha was a shit for talking to him that way. The man was dead.

And I certainly wasn't used to talking to people about their ex-spouses, as creepy as that sounded. But I'd spent enough time at the senior center during my grandfather's final years that I'd heard it all. Although, this was different. Noah hadn't had a long life with his one true love. Death thwarted that. At least the long-life part. I was beginning to wonder about the one-true-love bit.

"Is it okay if I ask how he died? I mean, I guess I just did, but you don't have to answer." I shoved the sandwich in my face before I continued on the path to uncomfortableness I'd just created.

"He was on his way home from work, and he lost control of the car." Noah continued to stir his soup. "He was on the phone. Not with me. But with someone—probably work, the report didn't say. And really, I wouldn't want the person to know. That's a lot of guilt to carry, even if it wasn't their fault. Steve knew it was icy. He was the one who made the choice."

I reached over and placed my hand on his free one, wanting to give him comfort but not knowing how. Even in his sorrow, Noah was thinking of someone else. He was such a good man, and despite what his late mate had said, he was a damn good cook.

9

NOAH

Cruz was too good to be true.

I didn't think it was all an act, but he knew exactly the right things to say to make me smile. How was that even possible?

Dinner went well, and we finished up the last of the cocoa from earlier before he finally had to head out. With his coat and gloves on, he paused at the front door and looked right into my eyes. "I had a really great time tonight, Noah. I can't wait until tomorrow."

Once again, I was caught up in the moment and practically flung myself at him, wrapping my arms around his neck and holding him tightly. "Me too," I whispered in his ear. "Me too."

I kept my eyes on him as I turned the door handle and backed up, opening the door as I went.

The bitter cold rushed at us, and we were both shocked to be staring at a wall of white.

Cruz took a step outside. "Whoa, that storm came in fast."

Autumn whined at Cruz's feet then backed up until she was inside the threshold. Even with her permanent coat to keep her warm, she didn't want to go out in that weather either.

"Maybe you should stay here and wait it out." I closed the door halfway, urging Cruz back inside.

He brushed off some flakes of snow that had landed on his coat as he came back inside. "Yeah, that's probably a good idea. I don't have far to go, but since I can't see more than a few feet in front of me, it won't be safe to get on the road."

"Then it's settled." I grabbed another log and tossed it onto the fire. "What's your favorite movie in the collection here?" I waved toward the wall of DVDs. "I noticed some good ones in there, but you can choose."

He smiled. "You're the guest, so you should choose."

I shook my head. "Nope, tonight, you're my guest. So you get to choose."

Cruz sighed then walked to the shelf with all the movies. "How about I choose three, and you can pick which one we start with."

"Deal." I cocked my head and thought about what kind of snacks were in the kitchen. "Did we use up all the popcorn on the garland?"

Cruz shook his head as he pulled out his first movie option. "Nope. There's a whole box still in there."

"Perfect. I'll get the popcorn going while you make your selections." I left him perusing the movies while I threw two bags of popcorn into the microwave. By the time I went back out into the living room, Cruz was curled up on the couch with a blanket, and there were three movie boxes displayed on the coffee table.

"I did my part." He waved his arm over the movies. "Now you get to pick."

"Okay, okay. A deal's a deal." I handed him the bowl of popcorn as I looked at each of the movies. Die Hard, While You Were Sleeping, and You've Got Mail. "We got some good ones in here. I think I'm gonna eliminate

Die Hard off the bat because being out here, alone in the woods, maybe isn't the right time to watch a terrorist movie.

"Fair enough." Cruz smiled as I put that box down.

"You've Got Mail is great for laughs, but I think we should start with While You Were Sleeping."

"Excellent choice." Cruz held up the second blanket in one hand then reached for the movie case with the other. "I had a feeling you might choose that, so it's already cued up in the DVD player."

My jaw dropped. "No, it's not."

He just grinned and hit the button on the remote to begin playing it. And sure as shit, the movie I selected started up.

"Seriously, how did you know I was going to pick that? I like all those movies." He had only known me for a few days. There was no way he could reasonably anticipate what kind of movie I'd be in the mood for.

"I had a 33% chance of guessing right, and I figured if you went a different way, I would just put in the other movie and you'd never know about my mistake." He shrugged and then placed his hand on my shoulder, gently rubbing the skin around my neckband with his thumb. "But this felt like the kind of night that might be better suited for a drama, so I took the chance."

A shiver ran down my spine as his touch warmed me all over. "I'm glad you did."

We not only finished the first movie, but we were at least halfway through You've Got Mail when I dozed off. If it hadn't been for Autumn snoring, I would have stayed asleep until morning. But when I heard her grumbly breathing, I opened my eyes.

That was when I realized I was draped across Cruz's lap, and his arm was locked over my waist, holding me in place.

For a split second, I considered getting up and going to my bed.

But my body refused to move. I was too comfortable, too happy in his arms, to even move an inch. I didn't want to disturb him, and I definitely didn't want him to wake up and scoot away from me.

It was just one night.

I could allow myself to be happy and comfortable with another alpha for just one night.

10

CRUZ

It was official. There was no better place to be than wrapped in Noah's arms. Or was he wrapped in mine? It didn't matter. Our bodies were intertwined on the couch, and it was fan-freaking-tastic. But it was also something neither of us intended to do, and boundaries were crossed.

I cracked my eyes and saw Noah looking at me with a sleepy smile on his face.

"Sorry. I didn't mean to—"

He cut me off, his eyes closed and head shaking. "Don't...don't apologize. Please don't apologize. I liked waking up like this, and I slept so amazingly. I can't stand to think that you're sorry. Please don't be sorry."

"Shh." I ran my hand down his back, hating the inner turmoil he was feeling. "I'm sorry I overstepped and that we hadn't talked about it first. I'm not sorry to be here. I liked waking up with you in my arms too."

"I really liked it." He nestled in closer, his leg suddenly twitching. "Autumn." He giggled in my arms.

"Sorry. She probably needs to go out." Reluctantly, I extracted myself from my place on the couch. I didn't want to get up, but I really didn't want to clean up dog mess. "Come on, Autumn. Let's take care of morning business."

I'd known it was snowing hard when we started the movie, but I assumed it wouldn't last long. There was nothing in the forecast other than flurries. When I opened the door to let Autumn out, I realized how wrong that assumption was.

"Autumn, do the best you can, girl." I pet her head, then she dashed out to the porch before making a running leap into the snow. "Noah, the snow didn't slow down," I called behind me. "There's quite a bit out here."

He got up and padded over to me. Both of us stood in the open doorway, waiting for Autumn. She was difficult to see because her fur blended into the snow.

"That's got to be a few feet." He rubbed his eyes. "That'll take some time to shovel."

I whistled and Autumn came back onto the porch, shaking off the snow and splattering us both.

"It's up to the top of the steps. We're looking at maybe three feet in spots, depending on the drift." I had a snowblower in the outbuilding, but getting to it was going to be the challenge. So much snow.

If Autumn had been any smaller, she'd have been stuck after her dive off the porch. She waltzed right past us and went inside as if to say, "You fools can stand in the cold." She was right.

I shut the door to keep the cold out. "I'll start a fire to help with the chill and put on some coffee while you shower."

"What I just heard is that I stink to the high heavens." He stuck his tongue out playfully.

"That's what I said alright," I sassed right back. "You're shivering. Go take a hot shower, and when you come down, the fire will be toasty and the coffee brewed."

He took a step toward me, hesitating before he took a second one.

I closed the distance and hugged him, loving that his body melted against mine.

He sighed against my neck. "Thanks. I wasn't sure..."

"I am." I kissed the top of his head. "Now, go. Let me make you breakfast."

He held on to me for another full minute, and just before he stepped away, he leaned in and I gave him a sweet kiss. There was no pressure for it to be more. Just a peck, really. But also...it was so much more. It told him I was interested but also not pushing. He just stared at me afterward, his finger going to his lips. For a split second, I thought I messed up, but as he turned and went toward the bathroom, I saw the bounce in his step.

The fire started quickly, and I was able to get the coffee brewed and some eggs ready to cook as soon as he came back into the kitchen. This would've been easier at my house because I had all the ingredients for a nice meal at the ready, not just the random groceries he bought for his week here. But this worked well enough, and if I used something he had planned for another meal, it was easily replaceable.

Replaceable after the snow was cleaned up.

I could get the driveway cleared with a few hours of work, so that wasn't the issue. This road was one of the last ones plowed, and with the unexpected storm, they were likely backed up with the main roads for the day.

My truck was great, but even it couldn't go through a pack this deep.

I'd probably be stuck there for at least another night. Thank goodness I brought Autumn. Poor thing would've been stuck at home alone.

"I have good news and bad news." I poured the egg mixture into the melted butter when Noah walked in.

"I like good news." Noah picked up the mug of coffee I poured for him. I liked seeing him standing there, hair damp and hands wrapped around his first cup of coffee for the day. It was so...homey and comfortable and...dangerous.

Don't get attached. I had to keep reminding myself that he was only there for the holiday. That was it. And he was fragile. No, not fragile. Strong. He was so strong. But also...he didn't deserve to be hurt. He'd had enough of that in his life.

"The good news is that I make the best eggs. The bad news...you might be stuck with me for another night. The roads haven't been touched, and this is one of the last ones they'll get to." I pushed the eggs in the pan, needing to live up to my claim.

"I didn't hear any bad news." He took a long sip of his coffee. "After we eat, I can whip up some food for Autumn. Growing up, my dog had to be on a special diet, so my dad made his food. I think I remember the basics."

I turned to him, my head cocked. "You would make my dog food?"

"Autumn gives hugs. She might not be just a dog." He shrugged and then winked.

"Are you thinking she's possibly a shapeshifter?"

"This is a magical cabin in the woods. Perhaps she's a pixie."

From what I remembered of pixies, they weren't that friendly. But I wasn't going to ruin his fun. "What makes you think it's magical?"

"I *know* it is magical because I smile here."

11

____

NOAH

I'd shoveled a lot of snow in my time.

In fact, when I was kid, the neighbors paid me to do their walkways and to dig out their cars. But that was nothing like what we had to do to get from the front door to Cruz's truck. He had a snowblower, but it was a bear to get to and then it wouldn't even start. No, we had to shovel it all by hand. There was a top layer of powder that was easy enough to lift and move, but as we got within about six inches of the ground, it was more like a solid block of ice.

And breaking through that was brutal.

We finally trenched enough of a path that if the main road had been plowed, Cruz could have headed home.

But he was sure the plow wouldn't be by before midnight, and there was no sense in him leaving when we had everything we needed for another day or two in the cabin.

Besides, I didn't want to be left alone.

When I first pulled up in front of the quaint little cottage, I was excited for the isolation and peace it afforded. But now that I'd gotten to know Cruz, I didn't want him to leave me alone. Especially if I could be trapped by myself for an indefinite amount of time.

"Would I sound desperate if I just come out and ask you to stay?"

Cruz planted his shovel in a pile of snow so it was standing upright. "Not at all."

I sighed and looked right at him. "Because I'd like you to stay. And, to be honest, I'm a little nervous about being left alone out here."

He nodded and reached for the shovel. "I'd like to stay too, and I definitely don't want you to be alone. Not tonight, not..." He shook his head and coughed to clear his throat. "At least we can get to the truck if we need to, but for now, let's head back inside and get warmed up."

I wanted to ask what he was about to say but I wasn't sure I was ready to hear it. I had a feeling he might've been experiencing some of the same confusing thoughts I had, and I wasn't ready to confront them.

"Oh, pine cones. These will look great on the tree." Cruz trudged across a deep blanket of snow until he was directly under a huge pine tree. "How many do you think we need?"

I carefully placed my boots in the footprints he'd just left as I followed him to the snow-free tree trunk. "Um, if we take the small ones, maybe a dozen?"

"Good call." He nodded and started to pile apple-sized pine cones into his arms. "These will fill in those last holes nicely."

I had a hole that he could fill nicely.

My mind kept rolling into the gutter. Cruz was just too irresistible. As hard as I tried not to think about how it would feel to have his knot filling me, the images and innuendos just kept coming. *Coming like I would be if he even looked at my dick.* Ahh, I was incorrigible.

His eyes narrowed in on me. "What?"

"What?" I shrugged and bent down to grab a few pine cones. "I didn't say anything."

He grinned. "What are you thinking about?"

"What? Nothing. I'm not. I just like pine cones. What's the big deal?" It felt like flames were licking up my neck with the flush of embarrassment taking over.

Now Cruz chuckled. "Sorry, my mistake. I thought maybe you were thinking about something dirty and that's why you suddenly seemed shy."

"Nope. Not me." My eyes went wide and I shook my head. I held up a smallish pine cone. "Just wondering if this is big enough for one of the holes?"

"I guess I have a dirty mind, because when you say stuff like that, I definitely imagine different things in holes."

I closed my eyes and inhaled through my nose, trying to maintain my composure.

"I think we have enough. Let's get inside and get warmed up."

You can warm me up anytime. Dammit. I needed a cold shower and some serious distractions from the hot alpha who made my body sing with desire.

"Yeah, cool." I stuck the pine cone under my arm and turned back toward the cabin. "I'm just not really familiar with crafty kinda projects. I don't have the instincts you seem to have."

"You have great instincts. It'll be perfect." He reached for my hand to help guide me back.

Something had been nagging at me, and staring at the back of his head as we maneuvered our way back through the snow seemed like a safe place to ask. "Cruz, can I ask you something?"

"Anything." He took a wide step then stretched out his arm to keep his grip on me as I followed behind. "I'm an open book and you have full access to every page."

I rolled my eyes at his corny but very sweet metaphor. "Do you actually set up activities for all your guests or was that just for me?"

His grip tightened slightly on my hand and his shoulders slumped. "Okay, you caught me. That was just for you. I've honestly never put as much time or energy into a guest before you arrived."

I stopped walking and waited for him to turn and look me in the eye. "So why me? What was different about me?"

He shook his head and smiled. "I have no idea, but I could just feel that you needed...more than just isolation. It was like you were...waiting for something."

"I guess I was." My breath stuttered and it took a second for me to remember to inhale. "I didn't know when I arrived, but now it's clear as day."

"What is?" He stepped closer, holding my hand between us.

I smiled and looked down at our entwined fingers, unable to look him in the eye as I bared my soul to someone other than my past mate. Someone who felt like he could be my future. "I think I was waiting for you..."

12

CRUZ

"Autumn, it's time to come in." Noah patted his leg and she came running. She loved him, and while I was sure the yummy food he made for her didn't hurt, it was more than that. Dogs picked their people, and she picked him as one of hers.

And so did I.

When he said he was waiting for me, my heart melted. We might've only known each other for a few days, but it felt so much deeper than that. Maybe it was the snow and the magic of the season, or maybe it—I didn't think so. It felt too real.

"Good girl." He pet her head. "Do you want a treat?"

"Pretty sure the answer to that is always in the affirmative." I shut the door behind them. "I'm gonna need to restock your kitchen after the plows come through."

"I packed enough for a family." He let out a long breath and chortled. "You can still see my breath."

"Let me see."

He blew out a long breath and I leaned in, squinting as I did. "Huh, the only thing I see are lips that need kissing."

"Whoa, that's what I see too." We kissed long and slow, standing there with our arms wrapped around each other, but neither of us pushed to deepen the kiss. We just enjoyed the feel of our lips dancing together.

Autumn bumped me with her head once...twice...three times. I thought she got the hint and gave up until Noah stumbled to the side.

"I think she wants that promised treat now." Noah smiled as he spoke against my lips. "What if we ignore her?"

"She'll knock one of us over with her exuberance." I took Noah's hand. "But once she gets it, she'll leave us alone for a while." At least, that was the hope. I'd never dated anyone she took such a strong liking to. She generally loved everyone, but her admiration for Noah shone above all.

"I better go get her that treat then." He kept my hand in his and started toward the kitchen, letting it go only long enough to make her a carrot wrapped with cheese. Never had I thought of that combination, but Autumn was all in. "That's a good girl. Now leave Daddy alone for a bit so he and I can get to the good stuff." Noah reached down to give her some pets.

"Daddy?" I didn't hate the sound of that.

"I figured that's what you'd be called since you're her people. I wasn't calling you that...I mean, I did just now, but in my head, it's more like Daddy Christmas." His face morphed into a beautiful crimson.

My body had a different reaction. My semi was now at full alert. Something about the way he said that just worked for me. But then again, what about him didn't work for me?

"Daddy Christmas... Do I get a hat?"

"I was thinking less clothes instead of more...unless I'm reading things wrong. I haven't dated in...it's been years, and if I got it wrong, I might die of embarrassment. But also...if I read it right and didn't say something, I'd... I'll stop talking now."

I gently tugged on our connected hands, bringing him to my chest. "You didn't get it wrong." I kissed his left cheek. "I just didn't want to push you. But that first day on the phone, I knew there was something special about you. Then when I met you, I saw how wrong I was." I kissed his right cheek. "There isn't something special about you... Everything is special about you, and by some miracle, you feel it too." I pressed my forehead against his. "No pressure."

"There's a lot of pressure, Daddy Christmas." He took our joined hands and pressed them against his denim-clad cock. "The zipper is getting painful. I wonder if we can do something about that."

"There's nothing more I want than to scoop you up into my arms and take you to bed. But are you sure? We can take our time." I wasn't sure how we would make things work past his stay, but I was bound and determined to find out.

"Things I am sure of are that I want you more than my next breath, I feel a connection to you I've never felt with anyone else, and we are never promised tomor-row. Give me tonight."

I was willing to give him everything, but for now, tonight would have to do.

"I should be wearing my Santa hat." I scooped him up into my arms, and he curled right in. "But given it's at home, I guess this will have to do."

"I'll pretend you're wearing one." He winked and wiggled against me.

"That'll do." I pressed my lips to his forehead and carried him to the bedroom. "Oh look, you have fresh sheets just for me." I placed him gently on the bed.

"More like because of you."

I'd suspected as much and wanted him to feel okay about it. I guess my words worked.

"Hoping to get them messy again, but this time, with your help." He pulled his shirt off, slid to the edge of his bed, and started working on his jeans. "You better catch up. I'm over here mostly naked, slick and needy, and you're just staring."

"Admiring the amazing view." I traced a line down the front of his chest. "It's not my fault you're so stunning I can't break my gaze."

"You keep talking to me like that, and I'm gonna melt into a pile of goo." He dropped his jeans to the floor and stepped out of them. "Not saying I'll mind, but fair warning and all." He twirled his hands, indicating I should hurry and catch up.

I loved how he kept me on my toes.

I yanked my shirt off and removed my jeans as if they were on fire. A slow reveal would have to wait. My omega wanted to see what was under my clothes, and denying him was not within my powers.

13

NOAH

My heart felt like it was going to beat right out of my chest as I watched Cruz slowly get undressed. Technically, it wasn't slow...but it felt like the world was in slow motion as his bare skin finally came into view.

There was a thick tuft of hair on his chest that made me want to reach out and run my fingers through it. But my eyes were drawn lower, following the line of hair that led directly to his thick cock. It was full and wide, pointing straight at me and slightly bobbing as I stared.

It felt rude to stare but I couldn't tear my eyes away from it. Steve had been well endowed, at least I thought he was. But Cruz was like a whole new level of magnitude. "Wow..."

As I watched, his wide hand slid down the length of his cock and cupped his balls. "See what you do to me."

Suddenly self-conscious, I dropped my hands onto my lap, hiding my own much smaller erection.

Ever observant, Cruz stepped toward me and lifted my hands up. "I hope you're not trying to hide from me."

My head shook, but he could see the truth in my eyes. "I'm just a little...intimidated. You're really big."

He pressed against my shoulders until I was lying on my back on the mattress, fully on display to him. "What I see is a perfect and beautiful and loving omega who makes my heart race and my breath catch and my balls heavy." He waggled his eyebrows, easing some of the tension I was feeling.

With a subtle nod, I exhaled and released some of the tension in my muscles. "Thank you for saying that."

He shifted his weight so his tree trunk of a cock was resting on my thigh. "I'm not just saying that. I mean it. You should be able to see just how much I mean it, but maybe I need to make you feel it."

My eyes drifted shut and I spread my legs wider, ready to feel it all. "Yes, please."

Cruz leaned down and kissed me, calming all my fears with his gentle licks and soft lips on mine. While his mouth soothed every fear and insecurity I'd been feeling, his fingers trailed down my side, across my belly and straight to my hard dick.

It wasn't as big as his, but it was bigger than it had ever been before. And when his huge hand closed around my shaft and began to pull, I thought I was going to explode into a million pieces.

And if that happened, I'd die a happy man, because this was the most erotic moment of my life. I couldn't even remember what sex was like before Cruz. I had always been happy and satisfied in the past, but the past felt like so long ago.

All that mattered was *this* moment with *this* alpha who was taking care of me like I was the only omega in the world. And my body responded to him as if he were the only alpha in the world.

When his hand released me before I could come and his face pulled away, I began to panic, worried I'd done something wrong. "What's wrong? Are you having second thoughts?"

His fingers combed through my hair and he gave me a gentle kiss. "Not at all. It's taking all my strength not to plow into you this second and give you my knot, but I just want to make sure you're okay with this. It's a big step, and once we take it, there's no going back. I don't know what that means, but I know I care deeply for you already...and once we do this, you're mine. So, are you sure you're ready for this?"

So fucking ready. "More than you can possibly imagine."

He hooked an arm under my knee to spread me even wider then positioned his cock at my hole so he could enter me. As if testing my capacity, he nudged forward, tapping at my slick opening.

"Please, Cruz! I need you." I didn't mean to beg but I couldn't wait any longer. I bent the leg he wasn't holding and tilted my hips so I could press over his head.

He moved forward at the same time and breached my opening, stretching me to the point that I was sure I'd split in two. But after holding in place for several long moments, I was ready for more. He held my gaze and waited for me to nod.

His mouth closed over mine, distracting me with warm kisses and his tongue teasing mine as he pushed all the way inside me. When his heavy balls bounced against my ass, I knew he was completely sheathed by my channel.

I took a few deep breaths while my body acclimated to his girth and length, and as soon as he did, I knew this was exactly where we both needed to be. My body had adjusted to fit him just the same way that my heart expanded to make room for him to move in.

And that was exactly what had happened.

Cruz had taken residence in the biggest part of my heart, a part that I didn't even know was there.

For the next hour, we rocked against each other, kissing and exploring all the new parts we hadn't had a chance to explore yet. And then Cruz finally did allow himself to release, filling me with warm seed that I could almost feel spilling out of me before his thick knot tied us together while I dozed off in his arms.

It was the perfect first time between an omega and his alpha.

When I finally opened my eyes again, Cruz was holding me with a whole new look in his eyes. "Good morning, sleepyhead."

"Happy Christmas Eve morning." I leaned forward to kiss his cheek, but I didn't want to scare him away with my morning breath so I kept it quick and chaste.

"What kind of Christmas Eve morning kiss is that?" He rolled on top of me and pinned me down with his massive body, kissing me long and hard until I was breathless.

It was amazing. "You're right." I sucked in a lungful of air then kissed him again, no longer worried about my breath. "That's much better."

Cruz chuckled. "If you think that's good, just wait until I show you my Merry Christmas morning greeting."

I rolled my head back as Cruz dropped soft kisses along my neck. "Sounds intriguing."

"I think you'll enjoy it."

It took some time for us to finally get out of bed, but when we did, we didn't make it past the kitchen. We made French toast and drank eggnog and made hamburgers for lunch for us and Autumn. And when it started to get dark, we ignored the fact that the plow had cleared the road and just added more logs to the fire while we curled up in front of it with cocoa.

It was the perfect way to spend Christmas Eve. At least for me it was. Part of me worried Cruz was missing out on family time because he felt an obligation to hang out with me.

I slipped my hand under Cruz's shirt, rubbing his firm abs. "So, what do you usually do for Christmas?"

His fingers traced a figure eight over my back. "I head to my parents' and see my family. It's a good time."

I sighed, the guilt washing over me at keeping him away from them. "You really should see them tomorrow."

"Don't worry." He turned to me and grinned. "We are."

14

CRUZ

"Did you think I was teasing?" I handed Noah a mug of coffee. It was Christmas morning and snow was flurrying around.

"I thought maybe you were caught up in the moment. You really want me to meet your parents?" He swallowed, his eyes like a deer in the headlights.

Concerned I was pushing him to go too fast, I placed my hand over his. "Yes, but if you don't want to be there as my significant other, I can easily say I adopted you for Christmas. My grandfather used to do that. We always had random people from his senior center there."

The first year, my family was a bit *unprepared* and we ended up scouring the house for a present to give to his friend so he wouldn't be empty-handed. We learned our lesson quickly, and now my mom kept a "present closet" stacked and ready to go. Filling it up over the course of the year had turned into one of her favorite things to do.

"Whatever is easier for you." He pulled at the hem of his shirt, not looking at me. I'd seen multiple sides of Noah since we met, but never one this hesitant, and that was my fault. If I'd done my job as Daddy Christmas right, he'd know just how important he was and how much I wanted him there with me. Although, it didn't help that I gave him the choice in the way I did.

He was probably second-guessing which direction I wanted him to take.

I cupped his cheek. "Oh, sweet omega. If I were to choose, you would be by my side as my mate. But families and holidays are a lot all at once, and if you prefer not to have that limelight right now, I get it." I placed a sweet kiss on his lips. "But just so you know, my mom will know the truth. She has that kind of sight. She saw my brother and his mate together the day they met."

My brother-in-law had been at my parents' house, fixing a drain pipe, when my brother stopped by to borrow my dad's jig-saw. The story was all kinds of adorable when my brother told it.

"I want that... To not have to pretend." He meant about us, of course, but it went deeper than that. Had he not come to my cabin, he'd have spent his Christmas pretending he was okay and now...he was. And really, he was strong, and he'd have been okay then too. I knew he would. If only he could see exactly how strong he was.

"Then you'll go as my date."

We stopped at my house on the way to grab the gifts I had purchased for my family and so I could put on my Santa suit. What's Christmas without your cool uncle showing up in a Santa suit?

"You really have one." He looked me up and down. "And it's taking all my everything not to take it right off you."

"Hold that thought." I handed him a few gift bags. "After dinner, you can strip me bare."

"Let's go." He pretended to race toward the truck.

I hadn't told my mom I was bringing a plus-one, but you'd never be able to tell by the way she greeted him. He was family. Done. That was how we did Christmas, and I'd never want it any other way.

"Let's get you some cocoa and cookies. Cruz's siblings will be here soon." She bent down and got her Autumn hug. "And I have a special pig's ear for you." Autumn licked my mom's face. She always spoiled my fur baby as much as she spoiled the rest of us.

We joined my father in the living room, our goodies in hand. He was watching Elf, just like he did every year. "Son, you brought a friend." He sat up in his recliner. "I'm Lenny."

"He's more than a friend, Dad. This is Noah," I said proudly. "He's here through the holiday."

"Then you better bring him around for a less hectic dinner so we can get to know him." My father turned to Noah. "Have you seen Elf? Best Christmas movie ever."

"I love the part with the revolving door. As a kid, I worried about that any time I saw them in a mall."

And just like that, my omega and my father were the best of friends. And when my siblings and their kids came, things were just as easy. We laughed, sang Christmas carols, ate, ate some more, opened gifts, and even played in the snow.

It was the perfect Christmas, and not even because the day fell out of a Hallmark movie. No, it was perfect because every time my eyes met Noah's, they were filled with joy.

"We can't wait to have you around again." My mother hugged Noah tightly. "I love seeing my boy smile."

"I would love to come back," he had my mother beaming. "And I love seeing Cruz smile too."

"Mom, I smile all the time." At least I thought I did.

"You smile because it's what you're supposed to do. It's habit. Today...your smiles reached every part of your being." She hugged me next. My mama was a hugger. "And you make him smile too. He even said so."

"*He* is right here," Noah joked.

"Get used to that," my dad chimed in. "And take some cookies with you. If you don't, I'll eat them all."

"But if I take them, I'll eat them...wait...forget I said anything. That sounds marvelous. I'd love to take some home." He patted his belly. "They were delicious."

"Let me get those boxed up for you." My mother pinched his cheek and then disappeared, my father reminding her not to forget the jello ones and the ones with the sprinkles Noah had loved so much.

"Thank you for sharing your family with me." Noah stepped into my arms and gave me a warm hug. "This was everything Christmas should be. I even got some cool mittens."

"You're welcome, my sweet omega. I'm glad you were here. In some ways, it felt like my first Christmas ever."

"I know exactly what you mean."

15

NOAH

I had to hold back my tears when Cruz said this felt like his first Christmas. Mostly because I felt exactly the same way.

Maybe not my first Christmas, but definitely my best. I had a great childhood and a family who loved me, but the Christmases you spent as a child in your parents' family were different from those you had as an adult when you were the head of your own family.

And for the first time, with Cruz, I felt like I had my own family. Even though it was just the two of us and Autumn, a sense of belonging and peace encompassed me in a way that I never thought possible.

It took me some time to accept, but Steve and I weren't happy.

What started out as fun and contentment, eventually morphed into resentment and distrust. In the end, he wasn't faithful to me and we were on our way to breaking up before his accident. I think it was easier for me to mourn the loss of him as a person than to acknowledge that our relationship hadn't been good for a long time.

But once I was able to look at the past more objectively, I could easily see what true love was supposed to feel like. And it became easier for me to see what I didn't have with Steve. He was a good man, and I'd always love him in some way, but I was ready to move forward with Cruz.

I was ready to pursue the kind of relationship and family I deserved. And even if I didn't fully believe I deserved it, Cruz would work every day for the rest of his life to make me believe that I did.

"I made cocoa." Cruz handed me a warm cup then scooted next to me on the sofa. "Are you feeling okay? You look deep in thought."

I nodded then sucked some of the whipped cream off the top of the cocoa. "Yeah, I was just thinking about...how perfect today was."

He slid his hand across my shoulder and gripped my opposite arm to pull me even closer to his side. "Yeah, it was pretty perfect."

I turned and looked at him straight on. "Did you mean everything you said?"

Although he had said a lot of things, he knew specifically what I was referring to. "Every word."

"So we're really doing this?" I bit my lip to hold back the grin that erupted every time I thought about my future with Cruz. "You want me to be your omega and you're going to be my... Daddy Christmas."

He chuckled. "I'll be your Daddy everything." He leaned forward and kissed me until we were both desperate for oxygen, even though neither of us wanted to pull away. "Forever."

I cupped his cheeks with my palms and silently thanked my annoying neighbor for wanting to use my house and sending me right into Cruz's arms. "Definitely forever."

"So...we should probably talk about living arrangements."

"Oh, right." I hadn't even considered the logistics of our remote locations. "You probably need to stay here to manage the rental. And it's pretty amazing up here."

Cruz smiled. "It is amazing. But if you need to stay where you're at, I can rent out my house too and manage these remotely. Or we can move some place in the middle, whatever you want."

Hearing those words just reinforced that I was exactly where I needed to be. I'd never really been the one to make decisions in my life before. Not because I didn't like making decisions, but because they were always made for me. Steve was the one who decided where we would live, what kind of house we would have, what kind of cars we would drive, and everything else.

But Cruz wasn't like that. He gave me enough room to have choices, without it becoming overwhelming. "I'd love to live up here. I think my job should be fine with me working remotely most of the time. I might have to drive back occasionally for meetings, but I have a few colleagues who don't come into the office at all, so I don't think it'll be an issue."

He seemed happy by that answer. "What about your house? Do you want to rent it out or sell?"

It didn't take me long to answer. That was an easy decision. "Sell. That was Steve's house. I never would have chosen it, and I have no strong connections to it. We moved there after I found out he was having an affair with our old neighbor." I closed my eyes at the memory of how difficult that time was. "We probably should have ended things then, but we didn't. So yes, I'm ready to sell that house and say goodbye to that time of my life."

"Well, then, how would you feel about spending the night at my place tonight?" Cruz cocked his head to the side and raised an eyebrow. "My real place. We can stay there for a day or two and then decide if we want to live there permanently, live here permanently, or look into something brand-new that is ours together."

"Oh, I forgot you have your own house here." I chuckled at how silly that sounded. "I mean, I know you have your own place, I've even seen it once, but I didn't really think about you being anywhere other than here."

"We don't have to go to my place. There's no rush for you to get the full tour. You only saw the good part." He chuckled. I'd really only seen the entryway when we stopped on our way to Christmas with his family. "It's bigger than this cabin, but needs more work. I've been slowly getting the little things fixed up, but it's definitely still a fixer-upper."

That sounded kinda cool. "Actually, I love fixer-uppers. I watch all the home shows and like to imagine having a place that I could work on with my own two hands. I don't know how much I'll actually be able to do with a hammer and nails, but I'd love to try."

"I'd love that too. So, should we head over now?"

Now? I guess there was no time like the present. "Yeah, let's do it."

It was a bit of a left turn to walk away from the cozy fire and head out into the cold, but it felt like the right next step. And I was done waiting for life to happen to me. I was ready to go after what I wanted. And Cruz was definitely worth going after.

It was a short drive to Cruz's cabin, and Autumn was practically squealing when we pulled to a stop.

Cruz rolled down the back window and she jumped right out, heading to the side of the house and disappearing through a doggy door. "I think she misses her toys."

"Aww, that's sweet. If I had known that, we could have come by sooner."

Autumn came barreling through the door with a stuffed hedgehog in her mouth. It made a snorting sound with every step she took, and her tail was wagging so fast I couldn't track it with my eyes.

"Nice!" I got out of the truck and scratched behind her ears. "Hey, girl. Sorry we kept you away from your baby for so long."

She chomped down on it twice in response.

"She forgives us." Cruz grabbed my hand and led me inside. "But I'm sure she'll want to show off all her toys before we head out again."

I followed him in, immediately in love with the ski-lodge vibe of this cabin. It was quite a bit bigger than the cottage I had been staying in, but the fixtures looked at least fifty years old, probably original from when it was built. "This place is really cool."

He slipped his hands in his pockets and looked around. "It will be once it's done. I imagined raising kids here some day..."

My eyes locked with his and held for a long moment. "Yeah, I can picture that too...and it's a beautiful scene."

16

CRUZ

"I don't hate this house." Noah walked his fingers across my chest. "The bed is especially nice."

We'd definitely made good use of it last night...a few times. I'd been nervous about him seeing the whole place, not because he would judge but because I loved this house, or at least the house it was going to be. I could have put all of my money into fixing it up first and worrying about going solar later, but I wanted to do the work on this place.

I couldn't even pinpoint exactly why. I just did.

How foolish I'd been. Of course he saw the house it could be. If things worked out the way I hoped, I wanted all the input Noah had to give. Hearing him say that his house was actually Steve's made my blood boil.

I understood why he mourned for his ex. That was natural, especially when everyone around him was telling him how hard it must be...blah, blah, blah. I'd been to enough funerals to fill in those blanks. They tended to be pretty universal and often came with a side of survivor's guilt for the person to dissect later.

And I hated to think poorly of the dead, but I wouldn't mind if Steve popped awake long enough for me to tell him what a horrible man he'd been and that he never deserved Noah.

"I think so too, especially now that I have someone to share it with."

Autumn jumped onto the bed, giving us both kisses.

"I think she felt left out." Noah scratched behind her ears. "Either that or she needs to go out." He rolled to his other side and climbed out of bed. "Come on, sweet girl. Let's get your business done."

She was off the bed and by his side in a flash.

"You don't have to do that." I sat up and stretched. "She's my dog."

"Is that right, Autumn? Are you Cruz's dog? Because I thought you were my sweet girl." He knelt down, allowing her to hug him. "Nope. She says she's mine."

"I guess that puts me on breakfast duty." My feet hit the cool floor.

"You don't have to." He stopped in his tracks. "I can make us breakfast."

"I know you can, but I want to. You can feed little Miss I-Have-A-New-Favorite-Person over there."

He laughed at my sassing and led Autumn out as I snuck into the bathroom. By the time they came back inside, I was already in the kitchen, looking for something to make. Sadly, the pickings were slim.

"Change of plans." I crossed the room and cupped his cheek. "We're going to my favorite diner for breakfast, then the home store to look around because...home store, and then I'll give you a tour of the town."

"I don't know about that." He pulled his bottom lip in with his teeth. "That sounds like an awful lot of the day in clothing."

I raised a shoulder. "Well, we should shower first..."

"If I help you with that, we can probably leave sooner."

We did not leave sooner.

But we did have a delicious breakfast, collected a ton of paint chips, and had a quick tour of town. It was late afternoon when it was time to drop Noah off. Only I didn't want to just drop him off, I wanted to spend every second possible with him.

"Where are we going?" he asked as we turned the wrong way at the corner. My house was on the left and the rental was toward the right. "Don't we need to pick up Autumn first? Or do you want to stay at your house tonight?"

Joy flooded into me, knowing that he felt the same exact way. "I think the cabin is better. It's kind of *our* place and it has food." I was only half teasing about the food.

"Then you better turn around and get our girl."

"I love you." It just came out. We hadn't said it before, always dancing around it. It was true, though. I loved him dearly, and he loved me. We didn't need the words, but fuck, I loved hearing them fall from my lips. "I love you, Noah."

"I love you, alpha. But if I'm being honest, I was waiting for the perfect moment to tell you. Like under the moonlight as we walked through the crinkly snow...or I don't know, by the fire?"

"We can do a do-over if you'd like," I teased, turning into the Tyler Farm so I could head back and grab Autumn.

"Nope." He popped the P. "I just wanted you to know that I've been thinking about it and that it wasn't an auto-reply to you telling me, is all."

"I didn't think that." I put my hand on his knee. "If anything, I felt like we've said it a bunch of times already, just not by using those three little words."

Autumn was waiting for us when we arrived, her hedgehog in her mouth. She wasn't forgetting that again. It was adorable.

Back at the cabin, the two of us made dinner and talked about everything we could think of. We had a lot of details to work out and not a ton of time. Noah's

Christmas vacation was almost over, and even though we planned to spend forever together, there were things that had to be done first, like dealing with his house and his job.

And then there was the nagging feeling that was growing deep in my belly, the one that said my place wasn't the place for us, this cabin was. And if we were gonna do that, we had a whole mess of other things we also needed to think about.

"Do you want to go for a walk under the moonlight?" I asked after the last of the dishes were put away.

"The snow is so deep." He swished his mouth from side to side, obviously unsure if it was a good idea. "We'll come home soaking wet, unless we get stuck out there and are eaten by wolves."

"Autumn is so fierce that the wolves stay away." She was anything but, and when she heard her name, she squeaked her stuffed hedgehog as if to prove it. "And as far as getting stuck...have you ever been snow shoeing?"

"Not since high school gym class. I loved it back then."

"That's when I learned too."

We got bundled up and put on our snowshoes. It was a beautiful night, and not too cold. We walked the property, checked out some of the tracks in the snow and under the tree where we collected pine cones, and then kissed each other breathless.

"I love you, omega mine."

"I love you, Daddy Christmas."

There was rustling in the tree behind us, and my head snapped in the direction of it to see the white tail of a deer.

"You see that," Noah whispered and leaned against me. "So beautiful."

The deer took a leap but never landed back on the snow in our line of vision.

Noah gasped. "Did he...he didn't... Did he fly away?"

"I can't tell you he didn't." Because it had been my first thought too, as ridiculous as it was.

"Did they ditch you? Are you fired as Daddy Christmas?" He took a step toward where the deer had been, smirking.

"Maybe." I shrugged.

"Guess you'll have to be my personal one, then. Their loss."

"My gain." And it was.

17

NOAH

"In or out?" I pulled my shirt out from the waistband of my jeans then tucked in one side. "Maybe half and half?"

Autumn looked at me as if she were considering the options.

"Yeah, I think this is better too." I ran my fingers through my hair one more time then stepped out of the bathroom just as Cruz appeared in the hallway.

"Damn, you look good." He looked me up and down. "Maybe we should just stay in tonight?"

"Uh-uh." I leaned up and went to my tiptoes so I could plant a kiss on his lips. "You promised me a real date, and a real date we shall have."

His arm curled around my waist and Cruz held me up to his body. He always knew how to calm my nerves while waking up every bit of electricity within me. "Fine, but afterward, your ass is mine."

I wiggled against his thighs, getting us both more worked up than we needed to be in that moment. "My ass is yours at all times..."

His strong palms grabbed it and gave me a squeeze. "Damn right it is."

When we finally got out of the house, I was buzzing with excitement. Every step I took was light and the drive seemed to just take seconds before we were pulling up in front of a restaurant off the highway that was twinkling with lights.

"Wow, this is so cute." It was like a Norman Rockwell painting. "Is the food good?"

Cruz held my hand as he helped me down from the truck. "I've never been here before but I've heard good things."

I stopped and looked at him. "Never? There aren't many restaurants in town. Where do you usually take your dates?"

He just shrugged. "Never been on a date before."

"Oh." I wrapped my hands around his arm and held him even tighter. "Well, I'm sure it'll be delicious."

As predicted, it was.

We had an amazing lobster bisque with lamb Wellington and pureed potatoes. It was like the most decadent meal I'd ever had. But the food wasn't the best part. Being the center of attention in the eyes of a man who treated me like the only omega in the world was what truly made the night magical.

"What can I get you for dessert?" The waitress refilled our water glasses and looked at Cruz with thirsty eyes. She was clearly after my man.

Lucky for me, he had zero interest. In fact, his eyes didn't glance her way at all. "Would you like something, babe?"

I smiled, knowing the endearment was for her benefit as much as it was for mine. "Well, the chocolate souffle sounds pretty good."

"Two souffles, please."

There was no way I could finish a whole one by myself. "One souffle, two spoons, please."

As soon as she walked away, Cruz reached for my hand. "You okay?"

"Yeah, just full. And..." I felt my cheeks flush. "Well, I want to make sure I'm nice and bendy tonight."

He chuckled and waggled his eyebrows. "I like the sound of that."

"Oh, you'll like the sounds alright." My dick started to get hard just thinking about what was in store for me when we got back to the cabin.

His pupils dilated and he turned to seek out the waitress. When she came by to check on us, he asked for our dessert to go. My alpha was always planning ahead. And he could probably scent that if he didn't get me into his truck in the next sixty seconds, I was gonna jump onto his lap and milk his knot until I couldn't think straight.

Fortunately, we managed to avoid being arrested for public indecency because the cake was delivered and he had enough cash on him that we didn't have to wait for a credit card receipt. We went straight to the truck, and instead of opening the front passenger door, he opened up the back.

"You read my mind." I climbed up onto the back seat and was already getting undressed before he was inside and had the door closed.

"I couldn't wait another second." His mouth was on mine even as he worked the button and zipper on his slacks. "I'm so fucking hard. I need to be inside you right now."

I didn't even pull my jeans all the way off. I got them to my ankles and then bent my knees to my chest. "Well, get in me already."

He smiled and then pressed his cock to my opening. "Brace yourself, omega. This is gonna be quite a ride."

He wasn't exaggerating.

I came three times and he was right with me for each one. I wasn't sure I could handle a third knot, but when he filled me up, it was exactly what I needed. And as his warm seed was locked deep within me, I could almost feel it implanting.

Like something profound was happening in that moment.

And through the fogged-up glass and the steam rising off our bodies, I had a revelation. "First dates are even better when you're with the man you love."

"I couldn't have said it better myself." He held me tight, kissing me gently as we both caught our breath.

And when we started to get cold, I rolled against his chest and placed my head on his shoulder. "Should we go home?"

"Definitely."

18

CRUZ

My phone sounded with the alert that was dedicated to the app I used for all things related to my rental. I opened it up expecting it to be a new booking for spring break, the next major vacation season. Instead, it was a reminder that my new renters would arrive in two days...two.

That was not enough time. Not even close.

Sure, Noah wasn't leaving forever. But he was leaving.

He had to go back to his place and deal with his job and the house and packing. There was so much on his plate. If I could've taken any of it from him, I would've, but aside from packing up his stuff, he had to deal with it on his own.

And that sucked.

I wanted to take care of him, protect him, and make everything easier. Instead, I was about to say good-bye to him for at least a few weeks, and I didn't want to.

"Maybe someone will buy his house the day it goes on the market."

Autumn was listening to me intently, and not at all because I had a bag of dog treats in my hand from the trip I'd just made to the store. No, she was just riveted by my story telling.

"We should be there now." On that topic, I knew she agreed.

Noah had a last-minute work thing come up that he was doing remotely from the cabin, and I left to give him space to do so. But I was itching to get back. We only had one more full day together. And it wasn't just that the cabin was being rented, because I would have loved to have him under my roof.

It was life.

"He'll call when he's done." I opened up the bag of treats and gave her one. "I wasn't going to open these today." Like I could deny her.

My mind kept wandering back to the jewelry store in the strip mall with the supermarket. It had always been there, of course, but I'd never paid it much attention. Then today, they had balloons all over the place and my eyes were drawn to it. At first because of the balloons, but then because of what they sold.

Jewelry.

Rings, to be specific. Engagement rings to be super specific.

"Autumn, I'll be back. I have a thing to do."

Ten minutes later, I was walking into the jeweler, not even sure what kind of ring I was looking for. Noah worked a desk job, so I didn't need to deal with the safety aspects of rings. I loved that they had silicone rings for people who did, but they didn't feel right for Noah, and neither were the ones with all the fancy etching. One by one, I figured out what rings weren't for him. Decision by process of elimination took a lot longer, but when all was said and done, I had the perfect ring.

The jeweler tried to talk me out of it three times, saying it wasn't special enough and or valuable enough. And he was wrong on both accounts.

A local craftsman had inlaid a ring with the most beautiful wood from a tree reclaimed in a local river. It was magnificent, one of a kind, and perfect.

"This is the one," I said firmly.

"Excellent choice." Finally conceding, he wrote my slip up and took my money. And really, at the end of the day, that was the trepidation he had over the ring. He wanted me to buy a fifty-thousand-dollar masterpiece. And if that was Noah's ring, I'd have found a way to do that. But it wasn't. This one was.

I still didn't have a plan as to how to propose or where, but now I had the ring and that was a start.

My phone buzzed in my pocket as I was stepping out of the doorway. Noah. Perfect timing. ***Done with work. Need cuddles.***

On my way with cuddles, I typed back quickly and added a second message asking him if he needed anything.

Cuddles was his only reply. Too sweet.

I swung by my place and picked up Autumn before heading over to the cabin. The house smelled amazing when we walked through the door.

"You're home. I threw a bunch of random things in the crock pot when I saw I was going to be working. It should be done soon." He crossed the room to me, throwing his arms around me and holding me close... too close. "Ow." He pushed back a bit. "Whatever's in your pocket should be marked pointy."

"My pocket?" I patted my chest, and sure enough, in the front pocket of my coat was the ring I'd just bought. Great. I hurt him with it already. "Oh, this." I pulled it out. If he already felt it, no point in trying to hide it, even if he didn't really know what it was. It just felt like a sign.

I held it out for him, and his eyes went wide.

"Autumn and I have decided that we want you around." I barely got down to one knee when she started to hug me. "Not now, girl. We need to get Noah to say he wants to be ours in all ways first. Then hugs."

She licked my face.

"I know you love him too and want him to stay."

Another lick.

"He needs to be asked first."

"*He's* in the room." Noah got on his knees in front of me...in front of Autumn who was in front of me, anyway. "And *he* says he wants to be yours in all ways."

"You didn't even see the ring yet." I snapped my fingers to my left, signalling to Autumn that her time to leave had arrived. "It's a really—"

He held his palm up in front of me with the ring already on his left hand. "It's amazing. It feels like...I don't know, like this place." He put his arms around my neck. "I mean, I'm more than willing to dissect that with you, if you'd like. But I'd rather be kissing you instead."

"I think that can be arranged." I brought my lips to his, pouring every ounce of my love into it.

When I headed up the mountain for my Christmas escape, I had no idea what was waiting for me up at the top. But now that I'd found my Daddy Christmas, I didn't want to leave him.

Ever.

But I had responsibilities to take care of back at my house, and the sooner I dealt with them, the sooner I could be back with Cruz.

I contacted the realtor Steve and I bought the house from and asked him to pull together some comps so we could price competitively. It was more important to me that I could close this chapter of my life and begin my next chapter with a clean slate than to squeeze every last dollar out of the property.

Besides, just thinking about all the work ahead of me made me nauseous. As I slowly packed up the stuff I wanted to take back with me, I felt sluggish and weak, like every move I made toward leaving was physically exhausting me.

But it was temporary.

I had to keep reminding myself that this short separation would enable a lifetime of togetherness.

"How can I help?" Cruz walked into the bedroom as I zipped up my suitcase. His strong arms closed around my stomach and held me against his chest.

I closed my eyes and sighed. I didn't want to leave for a single day, much less a few weeks. But I could be strong. I knew I could. "I think I've got everything packed that I want to take back, so there isn't much left to do."

His warm lips pressed against my neck and then under my ear. "I'm going to miss you every second that you're gone."

I held my breath and nodded, trying to maintain my composure. "Me too."

"But at the end of the month, I'm heading down there whether you're ready or not."

The vice grip on my heart loosened just a bit. "I'll be counting the days."

It was a painful goodbye, but I finally forced myself to get into my car and drive away. The snow had melted and the sky was clear so it was a perfect time to leave, but it also seemed like there would never be a good time to leave my alpha.

I was just about at the halfway mark when my grief became overwhelming and I had to pull over on the side of the road and empty my stomach. As soon as I did, I felt better. But I knew that would be a short-lived feeling, and once I allowed myself to think about Cruz again, that same sick feeling would be back. "It's gonna be a long few weeks..."

When I pulled into my driveway, I just sat in the car for a while. Not only was this no longer my home, but it didn't even feel familiar. I'd lived in that house for years, but after just a few weeks away from it, it had become a strange building that I felt no real connection to.

A knock on my window startled me from my daydreams. It was Greg. "Hey, you okay in there?"

"Oh, yeah." I opened the door and got out. "How's everything been?"

"Good!" He walked around the front of the car and waited while I grabbed my bag from the back. "My sister loved the place. In fact, she's thinking about moving here because the weather is so much better here than up north where she lives."

"Well, this place is going on the market, so if you don't mind her living right next door, you can let her know."

Greg's jaw dropped and he held out his palms to stop me. "Whoa, what? You're selling?"

I unlocked the front door and went inside. "Yeah, I guess I have a lot to catch you up on."

Greg followed me in and we got comfortable on the couch while I filled him in on all the amazing changes in my life. He was surprised to hear that I had not only gotten over my depression but that I was about to move in with an alpha I'd only known for a few weeks. "Are you sure about this, Noah? I mean, I'm happy for you and all...but that's a big move."

The silly grin on my face was genuine as I thought about the life I was about to start with Cruz. "I'm sure. I've never been happier, and even just being back here hurts me all over. Cruz is the one. I'm positive of it."

He reached for my hand and gave it a gentle shake. "Then I'm happy for you. I really am."

GREG DIDN'T WANT to live next door to his sister, but the market was hot and I received several offers after the first open house. I selected a young family that had been living in a tiny apartment and really loved the yard and space for their rambunctious son. It made me happy to know that a new family would be bringing love and joy into the walls of the house...especially since I never would.

We settled on a thirty-day close, but my goal was to sell everything I didn't want and be ready to take only the things I really needed up to Cruz's house by the time he came at the end of the month.

It was the only thing that kept me going.

Since he had sketchy internet and wi-fi whenever there was a storm, we didn't get to talk as often as I wanted. And not being able to talk to him any time I wanted made that sick feeling come back with a vengeance. Some days were fine, but after the first week, I was definitely having more bad days than not.

Greg stopped by with coffee and onion bagels on Saturday morning to help me pack up items to donate to the local omega shelter. "I hope you're hungry because I brought lox too."

"I am, but—Oh, shit." I ran to the bathroom and heaved up the water I drank earlier. "Sorry, I'll be right out."

Greg ignored my obvious request for privacy and walked right into the bathroom. "What's going on with you?"

I leaned against the side of the tub and inhaled slowly, not wanting to get up if I wasn't done. "I don't know. I just miss Cruz, I guess."

He soaked a washcloth with cool water then pressed it to my forehead. "Are you sure that's it?"

I cracked one eyelid open and looked at him from under the towel. "What do you mean? You think it's the flu?"

"No, I don't think it's the flu." He chuckled. "You were having sex with Cruz while you were there, right?"

My jaw dropped as I turned to Greg. "What?"

"Well, were you?" He raised an eyebrow, waiting for my response.

"If you must know, yes, we were." A slow smile spread across my face as I thought about all the times he cradled me in his arms while I was locked on his knot. "Oh…"

"Oh?" He smiled and crossed his arms. "Now you know what I'm getting at?"

I pulled the towel off my face and stared straight ahead. "You think I'm pregnant?"

He sighed and reached for the towel. "It seems like you might be. Which means we need to get you a test!"

20

―――――

CRUZ

It was officially moving day.

I'd been waiting for this day for so long. Not really *so* long, but it felt like it, even though his house sold quickly. Partially because of the low price he asked, but a bigger part was because of an uptick in the market.

And I was grateful for that.

The stress of the move had been wearing him down. I didn't need to be with him every night to notice he hadn't been sleeping. He was exhausted every time I talked to him. Like fall-asleep-mid-sentence kind of exhausted.

I offered to go down and help him with everything, but he insisted it was something he needed to do on his own. And, in a way, I got that. He was saying goodbye to his old life. Not the good parts, because he would keep and cherish those, but the bad parts were being banished.

Life was too short for them not to be.

I brought Autumn to my parents' and borrowed my dad's trailer to hitch to the back of my truck. Noah didn't have a ton of big things to move because he sold most of the furniture, but he had enough that his vehicle and mine alone couldn't hold everything. But with the trailer, we could avoid hiring someone and the waiting that came along with that.

"Thanks for watching Autumn. I'll be back tomorrow to get her." I hugged my mom then pulled the keys from my pocket.

"We'll only return her if Noah is present. It's been too long since we've seen his face." My mother was a pro at getting what she wanted. "And don't think I'm kidding."

"She's not kidding," my father piped in.

"I'll bring him around." I gave my father a hug then stepped away. "See you both tomorrow."

"I'll make my famous peanut butter pie," my father promised. "And if you're good, I'll let you have a piece too."

That pie was my favorite.

Driving down was better than I thought it would be. My truck made good time despite lugging the trailer, but when I pulled up to the house, I was surprised not to see his car. I got out of the truck then went up to the front porch to wait for him. Within minutes, I was kicking myself for not accepting his offer to leave a key for me. I didn't think I'd ever be there without him, and until now, I hadn't.

I reached into my pocket and pulled out my phone to call Noah and let him know I was there. Sure enough, there was a message from him already, but the phone's safety feature blocked the notification while I was driving.

Went to the store. Be back in fifteen. The time stamp indicated it had come through almost that long ago, so I didn't have much longer to wait.

Less than five minutes later, he pulled into the driveway.

I walked down to greet him. "You're a sight for sore eyes." I took the bag he was holding in one hand and grabbed his other hand. "Let's go inside so I can show you how much."

He leaned into my side. "I'm all for that plan, but we need to talk first."

Shit, that sounded ominous.

"No, nothing like that." He gave my hand a squeeze, and we started walking. "I just... Um, you'll see."

I couldn't get to the front door soon enough. This felt important, and I had this knot in my stomach that made me think the sale might have fallen through. It wouldn't be the worst thing to ever happen, since there were other backup offers, but it would mean more time apart.

I was good and done with time apart.

Once we were inside, he shut the door and looked at me. "I just got back from the doctor."

"Are you okay?" I put my hand up to his forehead the way my mother used to do. "Do you need to sit down?"

"No, but you might want to." He took my hand and placed it on his belly. "I wasn't feeling well, really tired and always queasy."

"I shouldn't have left you to do all this on your own." I could've worked remotely from there if I was pushy enough at work. "All the stress you've been under. I should've shouldered some of it. I'm sorry."

"Oh, silly alpha. You being here wouldn't have changed a thing." He looked down to his belly. "I'm not stressed...I mean, of course I am, because I'm moving. But that's not why I'm tired. I'm tired because I'm growing a human."

"Growing a..." His words settled into me after a long moment of shock.

My omega was pregnant.

We were going to be dads. My eyes filled with tears at the sheer joy of it all. We were going to be married, and now...now we were going to have a baby as well.

That cancelled booking was officially the best thing that had ever happened to me.

Noah's face went from excited to terrified. "Don't cry. It's not your fault. We'll figure something out."

"No. Sexy, sweet, magnificent omega." I placed my other hand over his middle. "These tears are... I've never felt this much happiness. We're going to have a baby." I hugged Noah close. "Thank you. I can't even... just thank you. I love you so much."

"Not as much as I love you, alpha mine. You've made me come alive again when I was living in this dark in-between. And now you're giving me a family." He kissed me sweetly. "I love you so much." Noah stepped back and started fumbling in his pocket. "I have some-thing." He pulled out his wallet and what looked like a receipt. "I'll be right back." He ran out the door before I had a chance to ask him what he was looking for.

I crossed to the door to follow him, but by the time I reached it, Noah was running back inside, waving a piece of paper. "I found it!"

"Found what?" He reached me and placed it in my hands.

"It's a picture."

I looked down at the black-and-white printout. I knew from when my siblings were growing their families that it was an ultrasound, but for the life of me, I couldn't figure out what I was supposed to see. "Show me our baby."

He pointed to a little blob. "Right now, we can really only see the yolk sac—which who knew that was a thing. The doctor says it all looks good. I told them of course they do. You should see their father." He giggled at his own joke.

"Flattery will get you everywhere." I traced the blob with my finger. "This is our baby."

"That's our baby. Now, how about we get me moved? I can't wait to be under the same roof with the man I love."

21

NOAH

Getting settled into our home took some adjustments. Not because Cruz was difficult to live with but because I was on the cranky side of the hormonal scale during the first eightish months of my pregnancy.

As I hit the last few weeks, I was finally starting to feel more like myself.

My friends and family told me it was normal to be irritable, but bursting into tears when Autumn accidentally stomped on one of my favorite flower bushes was not one of my finer moments. Fortunately, Cruz was a freakin' saint.

He never once made me feel like I was a burden. In fact, he was able to anticipate my needs before I could.

When I was starting to feel thirsty, a glass of water would appear next to me. When I was hungry, a plate with cheese and fruits and crackers was offered. And when my ankles were bigger than my head, his magical fingers knew exactly where to rub to release the retained water and keep me comfortable.

And that was just how he took care of me with my clothes on. Every morning and every night, Cruz cherished my body in a way that seemed straight out of a fairy tale. A sexy fairy tale in which the alpha in shining armor couldn't get enough pleasure and enjoyment from taking care of his omega.

Because that was exactly how my life with Cruz was.

My irritability came on like a wrecking ball, but Cruz was always there to soothe my heart and my mind...and my body.

"I may have to sleep down here until the peanut has emerged." I propped my feet up on the side of the sofa and closed my eyes. "Walking to the room feels like a marathon."

"Your back will never forgive you if you do." Cruz slipped his arms underneath me and pulled me up against his chest. "So I'm not gonna let that happen."

I rested my head on his shoulder and sighed. "I'm gonna miss this when the baby comes."

"What are you talking about?" He carried me to the bedroom as if I weighed nothing more than a sack of potatoes. "You won't have to miss anything. Ever."

I sighed, wondering if I was just being emotional...as usual. "You say that now, but after the baby is here, we won't have as much time for each other." I sniffled, even though I hated how selfish I sounded. "And our attention will be on the baby...not each other."

Cruz kissed the top of my head then gently set me down on the mattress. He dropped to his knees beside the bed and nudged my head so I was facing him. "We can have twenty babies and I will love them and take care of them and give them the best possible lives I can...but you will always be my omega. And I will always put your needs above all else. Do you understand me?"

I smiled and ran my fingers through his hair. "Thank you for saying that, but I don't want to come before our baby. I just don't want you to forget about me."

My lips were crushed by his as he kissed me like he hadn't seen me in a year. "I could never forget about you, Noah. My whole world starts and ends with you. And as our family grows, the love in my heart will grow too. You'll never be an afterthought or hold a smaller part of it."

This time, I leaned forward and kissed him, capturing his mouth with mine and kissing him like it was my job. I would have loved to stay there for hours, just kissing my alpha until the wee hours of the morning, but someone else was ready to join the party.

The muscles around my stomach and back all seized up at once, causing me to buck forward in pain as I curled into a ball. "Ahh, Cruz. I think..."

"It's time!" Cruz pulled me into his arms again and carried me back to the front of the house. He bent down to grab my hospital bag then turned to Autumn. "Okay, girl. You're in charge while we're gone. No wild parties, because when we come back, we'll have your baby brother or sister with us."

"IT FEELS like it's happening too fast." I curled up as best as I could in the back seat of the truck as Cruz drove to the hospital. "The contractions are constant.

Shouldn't there be minutes between them? Like, lots of minutes?"

"Just breathe, babe. We're almost there."

When a gush of fluid poured out of me, I started to breathe even faster. "Just hurry, Cruz. This baby is officially done being inside me."

"Count with me." Cruz used the firm tone he reserved for when I really needed to be calmed down. "One. Two. Three."

I blew out a long breath and then joined him as he counted. "Six. Seven. Eight."

It was a great distraction, because by the time I was at three hundred and eleven, we were pulling to a stop in front of the emergency room doors and two nurses were lifting me out of the back seat and onto a gurney.

From that point, things happened fast. I tried to keep counting just to focus on something other than the excruciating pain shooting through me, but I lost count somewhere after two thousand. Mostly because that was when I heard a baby cry out and Cruz choked out a sob.

"It's a boy. Noah, we have a son." His forehead landed on my cheek as I tried to focus on the slippery baby being placed on my chest. "And he's perfect, babe. Just like you."

As soon as my vision cleared of tears and I was able to get a good look at my baby, I knew Cruz was right. I also understood what he meant about his heart expanding. I didn't love Cruz any less. In fact, I was pretty sure my love for him had quadrupled over the course of just a few minutes. But I also felt such a deep and intense love for this little guy squirming in my arms that a whole new batch of tears blurred my vision. "I love you so much, Cruz. You've made me the happiest omega on the planet. Yesterday, today, and forever..."

EPILOGUE
CRUZ

"Noel is fine," Noah said.

I didn't need to look up to know he was rolling his eyes. For the past ten minutes, I'd been fretting that our son wasn't warm enough, and the odds were good he was starting to sweat under all the bundling I did. We weren't even going to be outside for very long. "I know. But let's go before he melts."

"That's why you're in such a hurry? Not because you're anxious to vow to spend the rest of your life with me?" He leaned in to kiss my cheek.

"Both?" I shrugged my shoulders.

When we announced wanting a Christmas wedding, we'd been thinking it would happen during the general time period. Unfortunately, both sets of parents heard something closer to "Let's plan a Christmas Day wedding of epic proportions."

It took a great deal of effort to rein them in to a small family wedding at the cabin where we met.

We stepped outside and saw the little sleigh waiting for Noel, a gift from Noah's siblings and cousins. It was adorable and all decked out in Christmas garland. He was still too small to grab any of it or even remember this day. Heck, he was too bundled to be able to grab it even if he were old enough.

"Here you go, little man." I put him inside and fastened the buckle, adjusting the canopy to block the sun and any wayward flurries of the day. "You're the best little ring bearer in the history of all ring bearers." Not that he was carrying the rings, but there was a pillow in front of his feet that signified the rings because my mother sure loved traditions.

"I heard that." My brother came up beside me and clapped my shoulder. "And for once, I agree with you."

"For once? I'm always right." I stuck out my tongue playfully, feeling a little giddy. "Aren't you supposed to be up front, waiting for us or something?"

"I thought maybe I could pull the sleigh so you two could walk down the aisle all romantic-like."

The sparkle in Noah's eye told me he liked my brother's idea as much as I did.

"Walk slow." I glared at my brother with a stern eye. "Like, Wedding March slow."

"How about Winter Wonderland slow?" He was so smug when he was right...rare as it was.

We'd chosen the song as our own personal wedding march because it just fit better. As long as we were having a Christmas-themed wedding, there wasn't a better song.

My brother started walking, pulling the small sleigh behind him.

I took Noah's hand in mine. "Ready to do this, my love?"

"I've been ready since the first day we dug for pine cones under that tree. I didn't realize it then, but looking back now, I knew it all along." We followed behind the sleigh on the path shoveled out for us. It wasn't completely clear but enough to make it easy for us to walk and to still feel like we were isolated out in the woods.

We reached the tree and Frank from the senior center was standing in front. As a retired pastor, there was no one better to pronounce us husbands.

Surrounded by our families, we recited our vows, exchanged rings, and kissed under the newly fallen snow. It was everything, and there wasn't a dry eye in the crowd, with the exception of our sweet baby boy, the one person I was worried would cry.

"What's that?" one of my brothers called out, pointing behind the tree.

Everyone looked and we saw a white-tailed deer.

"Do you think it's the same one?" Noah asked.

"Don't know. Maybe." I sorta hoped it wasn't, because in my memory, the deer we saw was a magical reindeer and not a common white-tailed deer that we had in these parts. And, of course, that magical reindeer flew off to tell Santa I was Noah's Daddy Christmas and he was going to be happy now.

Noah bent down to unbuckle the baby from the sleigh, and he held him up, pointing to the deer. And, just like last time, it took a leap but we couldn't see it land. Was it the location? A logical person would say that was it. But this was true love and a Christmas wedding and family, and there was no room for logic here.

There was a collective "whoa" from behind us, followed by all the nieces and nephews running in the direction of where the deer had been. Whispers of Santa filled the air and parents had to run to gather up their kiddos.

"It was him that day." I wrapped my arm around my husband and son. "It really was."

"How could it not be?" Noah leaned into me. "Only Christmas magic could explain that unexpected snowstorm."

"Only Christmas magic could explain just how lucky I was to have found you." I squeezed him a little tighter. "I love you, omega mine."

"As I love you."

Once the deer was deemed gone, the kids all came barrelling back, asking about the cookie-decorating portion of the festivities. Apparently, they were done with both Santa-hunting and being outside.

We all went in and decorated cookies before singing Christmas carols. Then, we ate enough food for ten families, laughing through the meal until it was time to rip open gifts. And when they were done, the kids all dozed off while watching Elf.

"We should be wedding planners." My mom beamed over her accomplishment as the credits started to roll. "Everyone should have a wedding day this amazing."

"Agreed." Noah snuggled in closer to me.

And they were both right.

Everyone did deserve a wedding day as amazing as ours, and somehow, we were the ones lucky enough to have it.

Or maybe it wasn't luck.

Maybe it was Christmas magic.

THE
MISTLETOE
PROMISE
An MM Nonshifter Mpreg Christmas Romance
ARIA GRACE
LORELEI M. HART

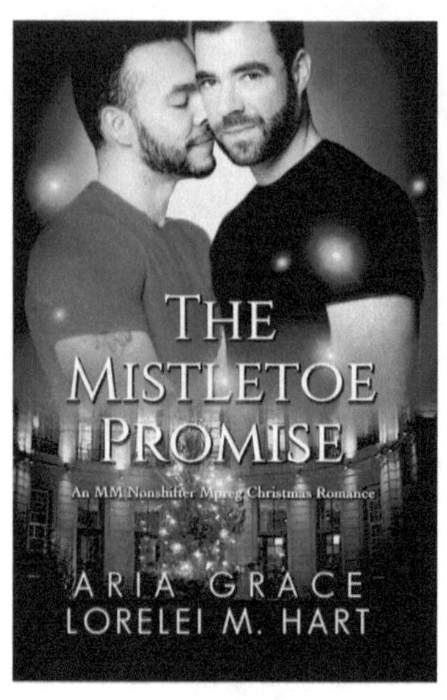

Order Now